"But you don't want to get married." It was a statement, not a question.

A shadow passed through Logan's gaze like a background figure moving across a stage. He turned back to face the view from the windows; there might as well have been a keep-away sign printed on his back. It seemed a decade before he spoke. "No." His tone had a note of finality that made something in Layla's chest tighten.

The thought of him marrying someone one day had niggled at her like a mild toothache. She could ignore it mostly, but now and again a sharp jab would catch her off guard. "What about a marriage of convenience? You could find someone who would agree to marry you just long enough to fulfill the terms of the will."

One of his dark eyebrows rose in a cynical arc above his left eye. "Are you volunteering for the role as my paper bride?"

Conveniently Wed!

Conveniently wedded, passionately bedded!

Whether there's a debt to be paid, a will to be obeyed or a business to be saved...she's got no choice but to say, "I do!"

But these billionaire bridegrooms have got another think coming if they imagine marriage will be that easy...

Soon their convenient brides become the objects of inconvenient desire!

Find out what happens after the vows in:

Contracted as His Cinderella Bride
by Heidi Rice

Shock Marriage for the Powerful Spaniard
by Cathy Williams

The Innocent's Emergency Wedding
by Natalie Anderson

His Contract Christmas Bride by Sharon Kendrick

The Greek's Surprise Christmas Bride
by Lynne Graham

Look for more Conveniently Wed! stories coming soon!

Melanie Milburne

BILLIONAIRE'S WIFE
ON PAPER

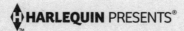

Recycling programs
for this product may
not exist in your area.

ISBN-13: 978-1-335-14821-6

Billionaire's Wife on Paper

First North American publication 2019

Copyright © 2019 by Melanie Milburne

Printed in U.S.A.

www.Harlequin.com

Melanie Milburne read her first Harlequin novel at the age of seventeen, in between studying for her final exams. After completing a master's degree in education, she decided to write a novel, and thus her career as a romance author was born. Melanie is an ambassador for the Australian Childhood Foundation and a keen dog lover and trainer. She enjoys long walks in the Tasmanian bush. In 2015 Melanie won the HOLT Medallion, a prestigious award honoring outstanding literary talent.

Books by Melanie Milburne

Harlequin Presents

The Tycoon's Marriage Deal
A Virgin for a Vow
Blackmailed into the Marriage Bed
Tycoon's Forbidden Cinderella

Conveniently Wed!

Bound by a One-Night Vow
Penniless Virgin to Sicilian's Bride

One Night With Consequences

A Ring for the Greek's Baby

Secret Heirs of Billionaires

Cinderella's Scandalous Secret

The Scandal Before the Wedding

Claimed for the Billionaire's Convenience
The Venetian One-Night Baby

Visit the Author Profile page
at Harlequin.com for more titles.

To my darling little black poodle Gonzo, who sadly passed away during the writing of this novel. I miss you sleeping on the sofa behind me in my office while I write. I miss your ebullient nature and zest for life, as if you always knew, like us, that it wasn't going to be a long one. Your life may have been short, but you have left love footprints all over our hearts. Rest in peace. No more seizures now.

CHAPTER ONE

LAYLA CAMPBELL WAS placing dust sheets on the furniture in the now deserted northern wing of Bellbrae Castle when she heard the sound of a firm footfall on the stairs. Goosebumps peppered her skin like Braille and a cold draught of air circled her ankles like the ghost of a long-dead cat.

No such things as ghosts. No such things as ghosts.

Her old childhood chant wasn't working any better than when she had first come to live in the Scottish Highlands castle as a frightened and lonely twelve-year-old orphan. Taken in by her great-aunt, who had worked as housekeeper for the super-wealthy aristocratic McLaughlin family, Layla had been raised in the kitchen and corridors of the castle. In the early days, downstairs had been her only domain, upstairs out of bounds. And not just because of her limp. Upstairs had been another world—a world in which she did not and could not ever belong.

'Is anyone th-there?' Her voice echoed in the silence, her heart thumping so loudly she could hear it booming in her ears. Who would be coming up to the north tower at this time of day? Logan, the new heir to the estate, was working abroad in Italy, and last time Layla had heard, Logan's younger brother Robbie was doing a casino crawl in the US. Fear crept up her spine with ice-cube-clad feet, her breathing coming to a halt when a tall figure materialised out of the shadows.

'Layla?' Logan McLaughlin said, with a heavy frown. 'What are you doing up here?'

Layla clasped her hand against her pounding chest, sure her heart was going to punch its way out of her body and land at his Italian-leather-covered feet. 'You didn't half give me a fright. Aunt Elsie told me you wouldn't be back until November. Aren't you supposed to be working in Tuscany this month?'

She hadn't seen him since his grandfather's funeral in September. And she figured he hadn't seen *her* even then. Layla had tried to offer her condolences a couple of times before and after his grandfather's service and at the wake, but she'd been busy helping her great-aunt with the catering and Logan had left before she could get a chance to speak to him in private.

But the upstairs-downstairs thing had always coloured her relationship with the McLaughlins.

Logan and his brother and grandfather were landed gentry, privileged from birth, coming from a long line of aristocratic ancestors. Layla's great-aunt and her, by default, were downstairs. The staff who were meant to stay in the background and go about their work with quiet dedication, not share intimate chit-chats with their employers.

Layla could never quite forget she was the interloper, the charity case—only living there out of Logan's grandfather's pity for a homeless orphan. It made her keep a prickly and prideful rather than polite distance.

Logan scraped a hand through his hair as if his scalp was feeling too tight for his head. 'I postponed my trip. I have some business to see to here first.' His dark blue gaze swept over the dust-sheeted furniture, the crease in his forehead deepening. 'Why are you doing this? I thought Robbie was going to hire someone to see to it?'

Layla turned to pick up one of the folded dust sheets, flapping it open and then laying it over a mahogany table with cabriole legs. Hundreds of disturbed dust motes rose in the air in a galaxy of activity. 'He did see to it—by hiring me. Not that I want to be paid or anything.' She leaned down to tuck the edge of the dust sheet closer around the legs of the table and flicked him a glance. 'You do realise this is my job now? Cleaning, sorting, organising. I have a small team of people working for me and all. Didn't your grandfather tell you? He gave me a loan to get my business started.'

One brow came up in a perfect arc. 'A loan?' There was a note of surprise—or was it cynicism?—in his tone.

Layla pursed her lips and planted her hands on her hips like she was channelling a starchy nineteenth-century governess. 'A loan I paid back, with interest.' What did he think she was? An elder abuser? Exploiting an old man dying of cancer with requests for money she had no intention of paying back? She might share the genes of people like that but she didn't share their morals. 'I wouldn't have agreed to the loan otherwise.'

His navy-blue eyes narrowed. 'Seriously? He offered you a loan?'

Layla moved past him to pack up her cleaning basket. 'For your information, I have never taken your grandfather's largesse for granted.'

Feather duster. *Tick.* Soft polishing cloths. *Tick.*

'He allowed me to live here with my great-aunt rent-free and for that I will be grateful for ever.'

She shoved the furniture polish bottle in amongst the other cleaning products in her basket. She had become closer to the old man in his last months of life, coming to understand the gruff exterior of a proud man who had done his best to keep his family together after repeated tragedy.

Logan let out a long breath, still frowning like

he didn't know any other way to look at her. Story of her life. One look at her scarred leg and her limp and that's what most people did—frowned. Or asked intrusive questions she refused on principle to answer. Layla never talked about what had happened to her leg, not in any detail that is. 'A car crash' was her stripped-down answer. She never said who was driving or why they were driving the way they were, or who else had been injured or killed.

Who wanted to be reminded of the day that had changed her life for ever?

'Why didn't he just give you the money?' Logan asked.

Layla's old friend pride steeled her gaze and tightened her mouth. 'Oh, you mean because he felt sorry for me?'

Logan's covert glance at her left leg told her all she needed to know. Just like everyone else, he saw her damaged leg first and her later—if at all. Layla was fiercely proud of how she had made something of herself in spite of impossible odds. She didn't want to be seen as the orphaned girl with the limp, but the gutsy woman with gumption, drive, ambition and resourcefulness.

'No.' His tone was weighted. 'Because he was a wealthy man and you're practically family.' He moved away to look at some of the boxes she'd packed earlier. He peeled back the cardboard flaps of one box and took out a leather-bound book, fanning through the pages, his features set in lines of deep thought.

Practically family? Was *that* how he saw her? As a surrogate sister or distant cousin? At six feet four with a lean and rangy build, dark brown loosely styled wavy hair, a chiselled Lord Byron jaw and deep blue eyes the colour of a Highland tarn, it would be a crying waste if Logan McLaughlin were her brother or cousin.

It was a crying waste to women the world over that he hadn't dated since the tragic death of his fiancée Susannah.

Not that he would ever date Layla. No one had ever dated her…well, not since she was a teenager. And she deliberately tried *not* to think of that one and only date and the excruciating embarrassment it had entailed. From that day on, she had decided her career plans would always be more important. More important than trying to go to parties or nightclubs in short dresses and heels that drew even more attention to her leg. More important than being told by a guy she wasn't good enough. Could never be good enough.

Logan closed the book with a little snap and placed it back on top of the others. He turned to look at her.

Yep, with a frown.

'Where will you and your aunt go if this place is sold?'

Layla's eyes widened and her chest developed a tight, can't-take-another-breath ache. '*Sold?* You're selling Bellbrae?' She could think of no bigger tragedy…well, she could because she'd lived through one big hell of a tragedy, but still. Selling Bellbrae was way up there on the list. Who would she be without the shelter of Bellbrae watching over her? Her identity had been formed here, her sense of security and safety honed within the fortress-like walls of the centuries-old castle. 'How could you do that, Logan? Your grandfather left it to you as his eldest male heir. Your dad is buried here along with your grandparents and generations of ancestors. You surely don't need to sell it for the money?'

His expression went as blank as one of the dust sheets on the furniture, but his tone was jaded. 'It's not about money. I am unwilling to fulfil the terms of my grandfather's will.'

Layla frowned like she was in competition with him for Best Frown in Show. 'Terms? What terms?'

He stuffed his hands into his trouser pockets and moved to look out of one of the mullioned windows, his back turned to her. Layla could see the tension in his shoulders even through his clothes.

The breadth of his shoulders had always secretly fascinated her.

She had often seen him rowing and swimming in summer on the lake on the Bellbrae estate when he'd come home to visit. Tall and lean-hipped with abdomen muscles ridged with strength and endurance, she had been fascinated by his athleticism as it had been in such stark contrast to her young broken body. And when he'd brought Susannah home for visits, Layla had watched them both. Susannah had been supermodel stunning, slim and glamourous. Never had Layla seen two people more perfect for each other or more devotedly in love. It had set a benchmark for her to aspire to. An impossible benchmark perhaps, but a girl could dream, couldn't she?

Logan turned to look at her, his jaw set in a taut line. 'Unless I marry within three months, the entire estate will pass to Robbie.'

Layla licked her carpet-dry lips, her heart suddenly flapping like a loose window shutter in a stiff Highland breeze. 'Oh…'

He drew in a breath and released it in a gust of frustration. 'Yes. Oh. And we both know what he will do when he gets his hands on this place.'

Layla couldn't allow her mind to even go there. No two brothers could ever be more disparate. Logan was the strong, silent type—hard-working and responsible. Robbie was a loud party boy with a streak of recklessness who had already brought shame on the family too many times to count. 'You think he'd sell it?'

He gave a grim movement of his lips that wasn't anywhere near a smile. 'Or—worse—turn it into party central for irresponsible playboys like himself.'

Layla chewed her lower lip, her thoughts in a tangled knot. If Bellbrae was sold, what would happen to her great-aunt? Where would Aunt Elsie live if not here? Her great-aunt lived in a little cottage on the estate where she had spent the last forty years. Like Layla, it was the only home she knew. And what would happen to Logan's grandfather's elderly dog, Flossie? The dog was almost blind and would find a move to another place even more distressing than Aunt Elsie would. 'There must be something you can do to challenge the terms of your grandfather's will.'

'The will is ironclad.' He turned away to look at the view from the windows, even the sound of his feet moving across the carpet conveyed his disgust.

'Why did your grandfather write it in such a way?' Layla asked into the echoing silence. 'Did he talk to you about it before he…?' She still found it hard to believe the old man was gone.

Packing up Angus McLaughlin's things had made her realise how different Bellbrae would be without him. Picky and pedantic, he hadn't been the easiest person to get along with, but over the last few months Layla had made a point of ignoring his bad points and had found him to have a softer side he'd been at great pains to keep hidden.

Logan rubbed a hand over the back of his neck and partially turned from the window to look at her. 'He's been telling me for years to settle down and do my duty. Marry and provide a couple of heirs to continue the family line.'

'But you don't want to get married.' It was a statement, not a question.

A shadow passed through his gaze like a background figure moving across a stage. He turned back to face the view from the windows; there might as well have been a 'Keep Away' sign printed on his back. It seemed a decade before he spoke. 'No.' His tone had a note of finality that made something in Layla's chest tighten.

The thought of him marrying someone one day had always niggled at her like a mild toothache. She could ignore it mostly but now and again a sharp jab would catch her off guard. But how could he ever find someone as perfect for him as Susannah? No wonder he was a little reluctant to date seriously these days. If only Layla could find someone to love her with such lasting loyalty. *Sigh*.

'What about a marriage of convenience? You

could find someone who would agree to marry you just long enough to fulfil the terms of the will.'

One of his dark eyebrows rose in a cynical arc above his left eye. 'Are you volunteering for the role as my paper bride?'

Eek! Why had she even mentioned such a thing? Maybe it was time to stop reading paperback romances and start reading thriller or horror novels instead. Layla could feel a hot flush of colour flooding her cheeks and bent down to straighten the items in her basket to disguise it. 'No. Of course not.' Her voice was part laugh, part gasp and came out shamefully high and tight. Her? His bride of convenience? Ha-di-ha-ha-ha. She wouldn't be a convenient bride for anyone, much less Logan McLaughlin.

A strange silence crept from the far corners of the room, stealing oxygen particles, stilling dust motes, stirring possibilities...

Logan walked back to where she was hovering over her cleaning basket, his footsteps steady and sure. Step. Step. Step. Step. Layla slowly raised her gaze to his inscrutable one, her heart doing a crazy tap dance in her chest. She drank in the landscape of his face—the ink-black prominent eyebrows over impossibly blue eyes, the patrician nose, the sensually sculpted mouth, the steely determined jaw. The lines of grief etched into his skin that made him seem older than he was. At thirty-three, he was in the prime of his life. Wealthy, talented, a world-renowned landscape architect—you could not find a more eligible bachelor...or one so determined to avoid commitment.

'Think about it, Layla.' His tone was deep with a side note of roughness that made a faint shiver course through her body. A shiver of awareness. A shiver of longing that could no longer be restrained in its secret home.

Layla picked up her basket from the floor and held it in front of her body like a shield. Was he teasing her? Making fun of her? He must surely know she wasn't marriage material—certainly not for someone like him. She was about as far away from Susannah as you could get. 'Don't be ridiculous.'

His hand came down to touch her on the forearm, and even through two layers of clothing her skin tingled. She looked down at his long strong fingers and disguised a swallow. She could count on one hand the number of times he had touched her over the years and still have fingers left over. His touch was unfamiliar and strange, alien almost, and yet her body reacted like a crocus bulb to spring sunshine.

'I'm serious,' he said, looking at her with watchful intensity. 'I need a temporary wife to save Bellbrae from being sold or destroyed and who better than someone who loves this place as much as I do?'

But you don't love me.

The words came into her head at random but she had no way of getting rid of them. They were like gate-crashers at a party, unwelcome, intrusive. Forbidden. Yep, she definitely had to switch reading genres. Layla slipped out of his hold and moved a couple of steps back, still holding her basket in front of her body. 'I'm sure you can find someone much more suitable to be your wife than me.'

Someone beautiful.

Someone glamourous.

Someone perfect.

'Layla, I'm not talking about a real marriage here.' His frown was back, his voice as steady and calm as a patient teacher speaking to a slow student. 'It would be a marriage on paper and would only last a year, max. We wouldn't even have to go through the charade of a big wedding. We could marry privately with only the minimum witnesses required to make it legal.'

Layla rolled her lips together, her gaze slipping away from his. Her mind was wheeling round and round like a hamster on performance-enhancing drugs. A short-term marriage to Logan McLaughlin to save Bellbrae. To save her great-aunt and Flossie the geriatric dog. Layla would wear Logan's ring but not be a real bride. Given her dating record, it might be her only chance to be anyone's bride. Could she agree to spend the year being 'married' to Logan? Living with him for all intents and purposes as if they had married for all the right reasons?

But who would ever believe *she* was the love of his life?

Layla brought her gaze back up to meet his. 'Aren't you worried what people might say? I mean, the upstairs-downstairs thing? I'm the housekeeper's orphaned great-niece. You're the Laird of the castle. I'm hardly what anyone would consider a suitable bride for you.'

His frown carved a trench between his midnight-blue eyes. 'Why are you so hard on yourself? You're a beautiful young woman. You have nothing to be ashamed of.'

Wow. A compliment.

A warm glow flooded through her body, her self-esteem waking from a coma. Beautiful, huh? That certainly wasn't what her mirror told her, but then Logan had never seen the full extent of her scars. But a compliment was a compliment and she was going to take it at face value for once. She brought her gaze back to his, keeping her tone even. 'And what happens when the year is up?'

'We have the marriage annulled and get on with our lives as before.'

Layla put down the cleaning basket and wiped her suddenly damp palms on her thighs. She had suffered temptation before and mostly resisted. Mostly. But walking past a bowl of her great-aunt's Belgian chocolate mousse was clearly not in the same league as agreeing to be Logan's temporary bride. She would be in close contact with him, not sleeping with him but living with him.

Sharing his life for a Whole Year.

How was she going to stop herself from developing feelings for him? Feelings that were already lurking in the background like a secret smouldering coal that only needed a tiny whiff of oxygen to leap into a scorching hot flame. She could feel it now—the slow burn of attraction that made her aware of every movement he made. Every time he took a breath, every time he frowned, every time his gaze meshed with hers.

'I don't expect you to do this for nothing, Layla. I'll make sure you are financially well compensated.' He named a figure that made her eyebrows shoot up so high they nearly flew off her face.

Now was probably not the time to tell him she would have done it free. There was probably never going to be that time. Logan had loved and loved deeply and had tragically lost that love. No woman would ever take the place of his fiancée and any woman who thought she could would be a silly romantic fool.

But the amount of money he was offering would allow Layla to expand her cleaning business into a household concierge service as well. She could take on more staff so she didn't have to do so much of the physical work, which increasingly tired her. It would mean she could be at the helm of her business playing to her strengths instead of her weakness.

Layla raised her chin, keen to portray a cool and steady composure she was nowhere near feeling. 'I'd like a day or two to think about it.' She was proud of the evenness of her tone given the pitty-pat, pitty-pat hammering of her pulse.

His expression barely changed but she sensed a restrained relief sweeping through him. 'Of course. It's a big decision and not without its risks, which brings me to a difficult but necessary discussion.'

Layla knew where he was going with this and it annoyed her that he thought her so gauche for it to even be a possibility for her to fall in love with him. She was definitely no Jane Eyre. She might find him ridiculously attractive and her pulse might go a little crazy when he was around but that's as far as it could ever go. As far as she would *let* it go. She had willpower, didn't she? She would send it to boot camp ASAP.

She raised her brows in twin arcs of derision. 'Oh, the one about me not getting any silly ideas about falling head over heels in love with you?'

Heels? Now *that* was the stuff of fantasy.

If he was taken aback by her bluntness, he didn't show it. 'I would hate you to get hurt in the process of helping me save Bellbrae. We both love this place but it doesn't mean we have to fall in love with each other.'

Layla painted a stiff smile on her lips but something inside her shrivelled. Of course, he would never fall in love with her. Why would he? She was more or less invisible to him and had been for the past fourteen years. But for him to rule the possibility out at the get-go was still a slap in the face to her feminine ego. 'Message received loud and clear.'

He gave a slight nod, the quiet intensity of his gaze unsettling her already shaky equilibrium. 'Here—I'll carry your basket downstairs for you.'

He stepped forward to pick up her basket at the same time she bent down to get it. Their hands met on the handle and a jolt of electricity shot up Layla's arm and straight to her core, fizzing like the ignited wick of a firework. She pulled hers out away and straightened but in her haste, she lost her balance and would have fallen if it hadn't been for the quick action of Logan grabbing her arm to hold her steady. His fingers overlapped on the slim bones of her wrist and another wave of heat coursed through her body. Heat that simmered and sizzled in all her secret places.

His gaze locked with hers and she got the strangest sense he was seeing her for the first time. The slight flare of his pupils, the gentling of his fingers around her wrist less of a steadying hold, more like that of a caress. She could smell the cool fresh lime top notes of his aftershave and the base notes of cool forest wood and country leather. She could see the various shades of blue flecks in his eyes, reminding her of flickering shadows over a deep mountain lake. His lean jaw was lightly sprinkled with regrowth; the dark pinpricks a reminder of the potent male hormones surging around his body.

His mouth…

Her heart skipped a beat. Her stomach flip-flopped. Her female hormones started a party. She should *not* have looked at his mouth. But she was drawn by an impulse she had zero control over. His lips were more or less even in volume with well-defined contours that hinted at his determined, goal-achieving personality. She wondered what his mouth would feel like pressed to her own. Wondered and wanted and wished for it to happen.

'Are you okay?' His voice was husky and low—as low as an intimate lover's voice.

Layla stretched her lips into a polite smile that felt shaky around the edges. 'I'm fine. Thanks.' She stepped out of his hold to create some distance between them but she couldn't help noticing he was opening and closing his fingers as if to remove the same tingling sensation she had felt. Or maybe he hadn't felt tingles. Maybe he was disgusted…as disgusted as her teenage date all those years ago when he'd seen her damaged body.

'I'll go and see to your room.' Layla injected housekeeper briskness into her tone. 'I assume you're staying for a night or two?'

'It depends.'

'On?'

His unwavering gaze held hers. 'On your decision.'

'And if I say no?'

A fault line of tension rippled along his jaw and an embittered light came into his eyes. 'You and your great-aunt will no longer have a home here. Not if my brother Robbie has his way.'

Logan waited until Layla had left before he let out a breath he hadn't realised he'd been holding. But truth be told, he felt like he'd been holding his breath ever since he'd found out the contents of his grandfather's will. Nothing could have come as more of a shock than finding the survival of the Bellbrae estate was dependent on him finding a wife. A wife, he had resolutely decided seven years ago, he would never have.

Not after the suicide of his fiancée Susannah.

Logan went back to the windows that overlooked the estate. His chest ached and burned with the thought of losing his family's ancestral home. Generations of McLaughlins had lived and loved and died here. Every Highland slope and crag, every bubbling burn had watched him grow from baby to boy to man. Every tree was like an old friend. There were trees on the estate his great-great-grandfather had planted. There were gardens his own father had designed before he had been taken by pancreatic cancer when Logan was eighteen. Logan had learned the skills of landscape design from his father and developed it into a global career that gave him more money than he needed and fame he didn't want.

He drew in a breath as rough and uneven as Highland scree. There was no other way but to marry if he was to save the estate from his reckless and foolish younger brother.

And who better to marry than Layla Campbell, who had lived here since she was a child?

Logan would be lying if he said he hadn't noticed how beautiful she was. Perhaps not in a classical sense, but with her waist-length chestnut hair and creamy complexion and grey-green eyes, she had an ethereal quality about her that was just as captivating—maybe even more so. For years she'd just been a cute but somewhat annoying child lurking around the estate, spying on him and his brother.

But it was impossible not to notice her now.

But he would have to, because he wasn't entering into a long-term relationship.

Not now.

Not again.

Not ever.

Logan walked back over to the boxes Layla had packed and opened the lid of one that contained his grandfather's clothes. It didn't seem real that his grandfather was no longer here. He lifted out a Shetland island sweater and held it against his face, breathing in the faint smell of his grandfather's old-fashioned spicy aftershave.

If the estate was sold, there would be no trace left of his grandfather or his father. They would be gone. Lost. Erased.

For years, Logan had spent hours in his father's study at Bellbrae, sitting at his father's desk, reading the books his father had read, writing with the pens he had used—just so he could feel close to his dad. To hold onto the memory of his dad for as long as possible.

Logan put the sweater back in the box and closed the cardboard flaps, wishing he could close a lid on his guilt and regret. He hadn't been as close to his grandfather as he should have been. But losing his father on the threshold of his own adulthood had made Logan resentful of his grandfather's old-school parenting style. He hadn't wanted his grandfather to be a stand-in dad. He'd wanted his father to still be alive. He'd resented the way his grandfather had tried to control every decision he made, everything he did and who he did it with. It had been suffocating and had only made him miss his father more.

It had hit Robbie even harder and Logan blamed himself for the way his younger brother had rebelled. Logan had been too lenient with him, allowing the pendulum to swing too far back the other way to compensate for his grandfather's strict authoritarian style. But hadn't he always been too lenient with Robbie? Ever since their mother had left, Logan had tried to fill the gaping hole she'd left in their lives. But, of course, he had failed.

What was with him and relationships? Why was he destined to screw up each and every one?

But maybe he could repair some of that damage by saving Bellbrae.

He had been straight with Layla on the terms of the deal. Brutally straight, but he was unapologetic for it. He had no intention of hurting her by giving her false hope. A marriage of convenience was the only way he could save his family's home. A home Layla had loved from the moment she'd arrived to live with her great-aunt Elsie. If Logan thought his brother would do the right thing by

Bellbrae he wouldn't have bothered with the messy business of fulfilling the terms of the will.

But lately he'd become aware of Robbie's gambling habit. A disturbing habit that had run up some eye-watering debt. Robbie saw Bellbrae differently from him. He didn't have the same deep-in-the-DNA connection with the estate Logan had. Once his brother got hold of Bellbrae he would sell it to the highest bidder and walk away from the estate that had been in their family for centuries.

But selling Bellbrae wasn't going to happen if Logan could help it. He would enter a short-term marriage to protect a long-term estate. To protect the legacy his father had handed to him on his deathbed.

'Always do the right thing by Bellbrae.'

And he would do the right thing by Layla by making sure she had no illusions about their marriage from the get-go. He would pay her generously for her time as his wife. They would marry as friends and part as friends. He knew how much this place meant to her—how much she used it as a base when she wasn't in Edinburgh, where she ran her small business. Any niggling of his conscience he settled with the conviction he was helping her in the long run. He was offering her a staggering amount of money to be his temporary wife.

How could she possibly say no?

CHAPTER TWO

'BUT YOU HAVE to say no,' Layla's best friend Isla said on the phone later that evening. 'You'll get your heart broken for sure.'

'But it will break my heart to see Bellbrae sold,' Layla said. 'This is the first real home I've ever had. I've spent the last fourteen years here—it's made me who I am today. I can't bear the thought of it going out of the McLaughlin family. It belongs to Logan. It was wrong of Angus to make his will in such a way.'

'Do you know why Angus did it that way?'

Layla sighed so heavily her shoulders slumped. 'Logan has made it pretty clear over the years that he has no intention of settling down again. Losing Susannah was such a terrible shock to him—as it would be to anyone. I've overheard a few conversations where Angus insisted Logan move on with his life but Logan isn't someone you can tell what to do. Once his mind is made up, that's it.'

'So, he's made up his mind to marry you in a marriage of convenience?'

Layla pulled at her top lip with her finger and thumb as she thought about her conversation with Logan in the north tower. 'Yes, well, I think I kind of planted the idea in his head. But we both love Bellbrae and we both know how impulsive Robbie can be. He doesn't love the place the same way we do. He thinks it's boring and cold and too isolated. We have to stop him inheriting the estate even if it means giving up a year of our lives in a paper marriage.'

'Are you sure it's going to be on paper? Logan's a full-blooded man. You're a young and beautiful woman. Living together is going to test the boundaries surely?'

Layla affected a laugh. 'Calling me beautiful is a bit of a stretch. Anyway, can you imagine him being attracted to me? I'm hardly what you'd call his type. I'm not anyone's type.'

'You're way too hard on yourself,' Isla said, echoing Logan's words. 'You shouldn't let what happened in your teens colour how you see yourself now. But the whole friends-to-lovers thing can happen, you know. It doesn't just happen in romance novels.'

'I'm not sure how to describe our relationship,' Layla said. 'Friends is probably too generous a description. We're distant and polite to each other.

I sometimes think he doesn't even register I'm around now that I'm an adult. I'm like part of the furniture.'

'I just hope you don't get hurt in the long run,' Isla said. 'I want you to be as happy as I am. I still can't believe how wonderful it is to be married to Rafe, knowing he loves me more than anything. We're both so excited about our Christmas baby.'

'I'm excited about your baby too.'

It was hard not to feel envious of her best friend's happiness. After a rough start, Isla and Rafe had finally come together again and were eagerly awaiting the birth of their 'accidental' baby. But would Layla's marriage to Logan have an equally happy ending?

The odds were stacked against it and the sooner she got that straight and clear in her mind, the better.

Logan walked through the south garden at Bellbrae, the scattered leaves of the ancient deciduous trees crunching under his feet. The vivid reds and golds and bronze and yellows were like wild splashes of paint. The autumn air was crisp and redolent of the smell of cooling earth and leaf litter with a hint of the harsh winter to come. Each season at Bellbrae held its magic for him. The gardens and fields and Highlands beyond could be blanketed in white as thick as a pile of duvets and still stir him to the marrow. But unless Layla agreed to a marriage of convenience, he would have to say goodbye to this place. The land and home of his ancestors, the place where he felt deeply rooted to the estate as surely and securely as the ancient trees around him.

Logan waited for Flossie, his grandfather's old Border collie, to keep up. She was sniffing around the tendon-like roots of an old oak tree. 'Come on, Floss.' He patted his hand against his thigh and the dog slowly waddled over to him, her tail wagging, her tongue hanging out of her mouth in spite of the chill in the air. He leaned down to scratch behind her ears, a pang jabbing him deep in his gut at the thought of what would happen to her if Robbie inherited the estate. The old dog would not cope with a move to another home and Robbie wouldn't want to keep her.

Logan straightened from petting the dog and caught a glimpse of a slim figure walking through the archway of trees in the distance. With her wild chestnut hair and creamy skin and irregular gait, Layla looked as much a part of this landscape as heather on the Highlands. For years he had seen her moving about on the estate, reminding him of a faery or other mythic person. Touching her on the arm the day before had sent a shockwave of awareness through him—an awareness he found faintly disturbing. He would have to try harder not to touch her unless absolutely necessary.

The boundaries were not to be blurred and especially not by him.

Layla turned her head as if she had suddenly sensed him nearby. She clutched the front of her jacket around the front of her body and began to walk in his direction. 'I was looking for Flossie,' she called out to him, sweeping the cloud of her hair back over one slim shoulder. 'I thought she might have gone out alone and got lost.'

Logan met her more than halfway across the wooded garden to save her from negotiating the treacherous tree roots. 'I took her out with me earlier. Sorry to worry you.' He turned back to look at the lumbering Border collie. 'She's slowed down a lot, hasn't she?'

Layla bent down to ruffle the dog's ears just where his hand had been moments earlier, her hair tumbling from behind her shoulders. He suddenly had an urge to run his fingers through her hair—to see if it was as soft and silky as it looked.

He curled his hands into tight fists and gave his willpower a pep talk. *No touching. Hands off. Paper relationship only.*

'Yes, I noticed a big change after your grandfather passed,' she said. 'She misses him, don't you, sweetie?' She addressed the dog affectionately and was rewarded by an enthusiastic tail wag. Layla straightened and met his gaze. 'We all miss him.'

For a moment, Logan wondered if his grandfather had planned this all along—a marriage between him and Layla. The old man had spent a lot of time with her over the last months of his life. And his grandfather had given her that loan she'd mentioned. After all, she had been the one to suggest he enter a marriage of convenience when they'd spoken in his grandfather's suite in the north tower. Had that been deliberate on her part or just a throwaway line borne out of her love for Bellbrae?

And why the hell was he suddenly so cynical about her? She was part of the family—or close enough to being so. He couldn't imagine Bellbrae without her.

Logan had taken it a step further by suggesting she offer herself as his paper bride. He still didn't quite believe he had done that, but it had seemed a solution he could live with at the time. The *only* solution he could live with. 'Did you ever speak to my grandfather about his intentions regarding the will?'

Her grey-green eyes widened in affront and her chin came up at a proud angle. 'What are you suggesting? That I somehow put him up to changing his original will?'

Logan shrugged one shoulder with a nonchalance he didn't feel. 'You stand to gain quite a lot if you marry me. You said it yourself—the upstairs-downstairs thing.'

She coughed out a derisive laugh. 'Newsflash, Logan. I'm not going to marry you. It would be beneath my dignity to marry someone who's such an appalling snob.' She swung away to walk back the way she had come but Logan caught up in one or two strides and clasped her by the wrist and turned her to face him.

'No, wait,' he said, suddenly aware of how tiny her wrist was, tiny enough for his fingers to overlap. Aware too, of the bergamot and geranium fragrance of her hair. Her eyes sparked with chips of ice, her rose-pink lips tightly pursed. It was a mistake to look too closely at her mouth. For years he had avoided doing so. It was soft and plump with her top lip shaped in a perfect cupid's bow, with dimples either side when she smiled, which she was not currently doing.

'I'm sorry, Layla. That was crass of me.' He sighed and released her wrist, his fingers feeling strangely restless and empty when she stepped back.

She rubbed at her wrist as if he had given her a Chinese burn, her eyes still flashing. 'I find your accusation deeply insulting. The last thing I want is for you to lose Bellbrae but I refuse to marry a man who is so deeply distrustful of my motives.'

Logan had always secretly admired her stubborn streak of pride. She hadn't had the easiest start in life but she had made the most of the opportunities that had come her way after coming to live on the estate. She was a hard worker—too hard, he thought, given her leg—but it was a brave person indeed who took it upon themselves to tell her to slow down.

'I can only apologise again. It was a stupid thing to say.' He held her gaze, watching for any softening of her expression.

She appeared to be slightly mollified. Slightly, not fully. Her lips were still tightly compressed but the daggers in her eyes had been sheathed. For now. 'Apology accepted.' Her voice sounded a little gruff and she delicately cleared her throat and added, 'But there's another thing I find annoying. You're assuming I don't already have a partner.'

An invisible punch hit him in the chest and for a moment he couldn't take a breath. He'd heard nothing about her love life recently…in fact, he couldn't remember hearing anything about a boyfriend for years. But she spent heaps of time in Edinburgh these days with her cleaning business. She could have any number of lovers. And why shouldn't she?

'Do you?' he asked, not sure he really wanted to know. But a current partner would be a problem. A big problem in more ways than he wanted to think about.

Her eyes fell away from his and twin spots of colour darkened on her cheeks. 'Not at the moment.'

There was a small silence broken only by the rustling of the leaves at their feet as a cool breeze passed through the copse of trees. Some remaining leaves fell from the craggy branches overhead, floating down like over-sized confetti. *What was it with the wedding imagery?* Weddings were something he never thought of. He never even attended them, not if he could help it.

Layla's gaze went to the elderly dog who was now lying down at Logan's feet. 'What do you think will happen to Flossie if Robbie inherits Bellbrae?' Her tone contained a chord of disquiet, the same disquiet he felt about his ruthless younger brother's intentions. 'Would you take her to live with you?'

'She's too old to travel and I'm on the road too much in any case.' He exhaled a long breath. 'He'll probably have her put down.'

She gave an audible swallow and her wide eyes met his. 'We can't let that happen. She might be old and mostly blind but she still enjoys life. Your grandfather would spin in his grave if—'

'If my grandfather was so concerned about Flossie, then why the hell did he write his will like that?' Logan couldn't strip back the frustration in his voice. His grandfather's will had put him in an impossible situation. He felt cornered, compromised, blackmailed.

Layla's teeth sank into her lower lip. 'If I were to marry you, what would we tell people about us? I mean, are we going to pretend it's a real marriage, or—?'

Logan rubbed a hand along the side of his jaw before dropping his hand back by his side. 'I would prefer people to think it's a genuine love match. I'm not sure who's going to buy it, but still.'

Her chin came back up and the daggers were back glinting in her eyes. 'Thank you.' Her tone was distinctly wry.

Logan could have thumped himself for being so insensitive. 'That came out wrong. I was thinking more about in terms of myself.'

A small frown appeared on her smooth-as-cream forehead. 'Because of what you felt for Susannah?' She paused for a beat and added, 'What you *still* feel for her?'

Logan had never discussed with anyone the complicated relationship he'd had with Susannah. He didn't even like thinking about how badly he had handled things. It was better to let people think he was still grieving the loss of his fiancée, but in truth he felt guilt rather than grief. Gut-shredding guilt that gnawed and clawed at him with savage teeth and talons.

So many mistakes he had made, costly mistakes that had ended in tragedy.

'It's pretty common knowledge I never intended to settle down with anyone after Susannah's death,' he said. 'I guess my grandfather decided to take the matter into his own hands and force me to face my responsibilities as the eldest McLaughlin heir.'

The frown on her brow deepened. 'So, who will your heir be? Or will you eventually leave Bellbrae to a nephew or niece if Robbie has children at some point?'

Logan hadn't got to thinking that far ahead. His sole goal had been rescuing Bellbrae from being auctioned off to settle his brother's gambling debts. Marrying to save the estate was a big enough step, siring an heir was a giant leap he wasn't sure he was ready to even consider. Yet. He gave one of his carefully rationed smiles. 'I don't suppose you'd like to help me with that?'

Her cheeks burned a fire-engine red and her plump rosy lips flattened to a thin disapproving line. 'No.' Her tone was as starchy as a prim Victorian Sunday schoolteacher's.

'Only joking.' It was no joking matter but he refused to think about having a child. Hadn't he done enough damage with his brother?

Layla shifted her gaze, but he noticed her small white teeth resumed their savaging of her lower lip. 'I need to get back to help Aunt Elsie with something.' Her voice was not much more than a mumble.

'I need your final answer, Layla. Tonight, if possible. There are legal documents to arrange be-fore we—'

'I'll see you tonight. At dinner.'

Logan nodded in agreement. 'It's a date.'

It had been a heck of a long time since he'd had one of those.

Layla sat with her great-aunt at the Bellbrae kitchen table half an hour later with a pot of tea and freshly baked cupcakes.

'You're not eating,' Aunt Elsie said, pushing the tiered cake stand closer. 'Is something on your mind?'

Layla took a cake from the stand and peeled the polka-dotted paper case off the cupcake. 'I'm not sure how to tell you this…' she began.

Her great-aunt paused in the action of sipping her tea, her light blue gaze wide with interest. 'You've met someone?'

Layla only just resisted the impulse to roll her eyes. 'No. It's a little more complicated than that.' She took a deep breath and added, 'Logan's asked me to marry him.'

Her great-aunt's cup gave a tiny rattle as she placed it back in its saucer. 'And what was your answer?'

Layla wasn't sure what to make of her great-aunt's mild expression. 'Aren't you surprised he proposed to me?'

Aunt Elsie reached for the teapot and topped up both of their cups with the rich brew. She placed the teapot back on its heat protector before responding. 'Not one bit surprised. He's known you since you were a wee child. He's watched you grow up into a fine young woman. You'll be a good wife for him. Loyal and steady and stable.' She peered at Layla over the top of her bifocals. 'You said yes, didn't you?'

Layla nibbled at one side of her mouth. 'I'm still deciding…'

Aunt Elsie sat back in her chair, lifted the little milk jug to pour some into her tea and then set the jug back down on the table. 'You'd be mad to refuse, my girl. He's a good man. A bit on the quiet side but you don't want a husband who talks more than he listens. He'll take good care of you.'

Layla broke off a piece of cupcake with her fingers. 'He only wants to stay married for a year to secure the estate. If he doesn't marry within three months, Bellbrae will automatically pass to Robbie.' She put the small portion of cake in her mouth, chewed and swallowed, continuing to gauge her great-aunt's reaction.

Aunt Elsie stirred her tea into a small whirlpool,

glancing at her again. 'I know about Angus's will. He told me before he died.'

Layla frowned. 'And you didn't try and change his mind?'

Aunt Elsie sighed and picked up her cup again. 'There isn't a person alive or dead who could change that man's mind. Angus was frustrated Logan hadn't moved on from losing Susannah. Sure, he has casual lovers occasionally but his grandfather wanted him to settle down and do the right thing by Bellbrae. If marrying you is the only way Logan can see fit to do it, then so be it. You love this place and you love him.' She made a toast of her last words by taking a sip of her tea.

'Excuse me.' Layla gave a choked laugh. 'Not like *that*!'

Aunt Elsie arched her eyebrows. 'Are you sure?'

Growing up, Layla had idolised Logan from afar. He had been a romantic fantasy any teenage girl would have drooled over. But it was a bit of a leap to describe her feelings now as love, or at least *that* sort of love. Although…that tiny secret smouldering coal inside her was still there waiting, waiting, waiting for enough oxygen to fan it into life.

Layla looked down at the cake crumbs on her plate and expelled a long breath. 'It wouldn't matter how I felt about him. It's not going to be a proper marriage.' She pushed the crumbs into a neat pile and then glanced back at her great-aunt. 'It will be on paper only.'

Aunt Elsie's eyes began to twinkle like they were auditioning for a new constellation in the northern hemisphere. 'Of course it will.'

Layla gave an eye roll and stood to take her plate and cup and saucer to the sink. Her great-aunt was suffering a massive delusion if she thought Logan would be remotely interested in sleeping with *her*. She had seen photos of Logan's casual lovers. She had seen his fiancée Susannah in the stunningly beautiful and unscarred flesh.

How could she ever hope to compete with that?

CHAPTER THREE

LATER THAT EVENING Layla fed Flossie and let her out for a comfort walk. When she got back, the old dog began to snore almost as soon as she settled back in her wicker basket in front of the fire in Angus's study a few doors away from the kitchen. There was a pet door in one of the back doors off the kitchen, but Flossie was too arthritic these days to get through it.

It was sad to see the old girl's decline. Layla had only been at Bellbrae a couple of weeks when Angus McLaughlin had brought Flossie home as a playful and needle-toothed puppy. She had often wondered if he had bought the dog to help her settle in. She had asked him once but he'd dismissed the suggestion in his gruff and off-hand way.

Layla had spent many a happy time playing with Flossie, brushing her silky coat and taking her on walks about the estate, which had seemed so huge and terrifying when she had first arrived.

But with the company of the ebullient puppy it had suddenly become a home. A home she could not imagine losing. Her happiest memories—the *only* happy memories she possessed—had been crafted and laid down here at Bellbrae.

Layla was putting the finishing touches to dinner shortly after when Logan strode into the kitchen. She glanced over her shoulder and turned back to the pot she was stirring on the cooktop. 'Dinner won't be long.'

'Where's Elsie?'

Layla put the cooking spoon down on the ceramic spoon rest and turned and faced him, wiping her hands on her apron. 'I gave her the night off. She hasn't been doing so much cooking now your grandfather's no longer with us.' She waited a beat and added, 'She knew about the change to his will.'

Logan frowned. 'Thoughtful of him to share it with the household help but not with me.'

Layla pursed her lips. 'You might think of Aunt Elsie as little more than a humble housekeeper but she has supported your family through every high and low of the last three decades.' She whipped off her apron and flung it on the benchtop.

'When your mother left when you and Robbie were little, when your father died, when Robbie went off the rails that first time in his teens. And when your grandmother died when you were away at university. Aunt Elsie has cooked and cleaned and consoled everyone, working long hours and forsaking a normal life of her own. Don't you dare refer to her as just the help.' Her chest was heaving like she had just run up one of the Bellbrae turrets. Three turrets. Possibly all twelve of them.

He closed his eyes in a slow blink and sighed. 'All I seem to do lately around you is open my mouth and change feet.' He twisted his lips into a rueful grimace. 'I meant no offence. My only excuse is that I'm still reeling from being so much in the dark about my grandfather's intentions. I hate surprises at the best of times and this was one hell of a surprise.'

There were surprises and there were surprises. Layla could only imagine the surprises Logan had received over the course of his life were not the pleasant type. His mother abandoning him and his brother as small children to go and live with her lover abroad, the sudden death of his father from pancreatic cancer, the terrible shock of his fiancée's suicide and now his grandfather's odd conditions on his will. She could hardly blame him for wanting a little more predictability in his life. 'I hope you don't mind but I told Aunt Elsie about your proposal.'

Logan's gaze was steady and watchful. 'And?'

'She told me I'd be a fool not to accept.'

'And have you accepted?'

'Just to be clear—I don't want you to lose Bellbrae much more than I want to be your wife. Think of my acceptance as an act of charity, if you will.'

If he was relieved by her answer he gave no sign of it on his features. They might as well have been discussing the weather. 'I appreciate your honesty. Neither of us want this but we have a common goal in saving Bellbrae.'

Layla kept her chin high, her gaze level, her pride on active duty. 'She also thinks it won't be a paper marriage for very long.'

One side of his mouth came up in a vestige of a smile. It took years off his face and made something in her stomach slip sideways. It had been years, seven years at least, since she had seen him give anything close to a smile.

He approached the island bench on the opposite side from where she was standing.

'Why would she think that?' His voice had gone down to a rough deep burr.

Her gaze flicked away from his, her cheeks warming like she'd been standing too close to the oven. She gave a little shrug. 'Who knows? Perhaps she thinks you'll be overcome with uncontrollable lust and won't be able to resist me.'

There was a loaded silence. A silence with an undercurrent of unusual energy vibrating through every particle of air. Energy that made the fine hairs on the back of her neck and along her arms tingle at the roots.

Layla sneaked a glance at him and found him looking at her with a contemplative frown.

After a moment, he appeared to give himself a mental shake and then raked his splayed fingers through his hair, dropping his hand back by his side. 'I would hope you know me well enough to be reassured I am a man of my word. If I say our marriage will not be consummated, then you can count on it that it won't be.'

Why? Because she was so undesirable? So repugnant to him as she had been to her first and only boyfriend when she was sixteen? So unlike the gorgeous supermodel types Logan had occasional casual flings with?

'Right now, I don't know whether I should be reassured or insulted.' The words slipped out before her wounded ego could check in with her brain.

Logan's gaze dipped to her mouth, lingering there a fraction longer than was necessary. His eyes came back to mesh with hers and her heart gave an odd little thumpity-thump. She had to summon every bit of willpower she possessed and then some not to glance at his mouth. She wondered if he kissed hard or soft or somewhere in between. Her mind suddenly filled with images of them making love, her limbs entangled with his, her senses singing from his touch, his mouth

clamped to hers in passion. A passion she could
only imagine because she had never experienced
it herself.

'It would only complicate things if we were to
have a normal relationship.' His voice had a rough
edge as if something was clogging his throat. 'It
wouldn't be fair to you.'

Layla turned and went back to the pot simmering on the cooktop behind her. Her body was simmering too. Smouldering with new sensations and
longings she had no idea how to control. Had his
'proposal' unlocked something in her? Made her
aware of herself in a way she hadn't been before?
Aware of her needs, the needs she had ignored and
denied, always telling herself no one would ever
want to marry her.

She took the lid off the pot, picked up the spoon
and gave the casserole a couple of stirs. 'Will you
continue to have casual lovers during our marriage?'

'No. That's something else that wouldn't be fair
to you. And I would hope you would refrain from
any dalliances yourself.'

Layla put the spoon down again and placed the
lid back on the pot with a clang. 'You don't have
to worry on that score. I haven't had a casual lover
my entire adult life.'

Why did you tell him that?

There was another pulsing silence.

Logan came to her side of the island bench and stood next to her near the cooktop. Her body went on high alert, every nerve and cell aware of his closeness. Not touching, but close enough to do so if either of them moved half a step.

'But you've had lovers, right?'

Layla turned her head to glance at him, hoping he would put her flaming cheeks down to her proximity to the simmering pot in front of her. 'Not as many as you might think.' No way was she going to announce she was a twenty-six-year-old virgin. She moved from the cooktop to gather the serving utensils. 'I haven't opened any wine for dinner. Do you want to grab a bottle? We'll be eating in the small green dining room since it's just the two of us.'

'I'll bring something up from the cellar.'

Just the two of us.

How cosy and intimate that sounded, but it wasn't true. He would never have asked her to marry him if it hadn't been for the strange conditions on his grandfather's will. She had to remember that at all costs. This was a business deal. Nothing personal. Nothing lasting.

Nothing.

Logan spent longer than he needed to choosing a wine from the well-stocked Bellbrae cellar. He remembered the bottle of vintage champagne he'd selected when he'd got engaged to Susannah. How excited he'd felt, how ready he'd felt for the commitment he'd made. How he had imagined himself to be in love and Susannah in love with him. He had been Layla's age—twenty-six. Susannah had been two years younger with a host of issues he had been completely oblivious to until it was too late.

Losing his father after a devastatingly brief battle with cancer had compelled him to settle down as soon as he could. With hindsight, he could see now how many signs he'd missed about the suitability of Susannah, even his own readiness for such a permanent commitment. He'd had no way of knowing how that night of celebrating his engagement would end less than a year later in Susannah's death. How could he have been so ignorant of the demons she'd battled on a daily basis?

What did that say about *him*?

It said he wasn't relationship material, that's what it said. Or at least, not *that* sort of relationship. Promising to love someone no matter what, making a long-term commitment were things he could no longer do. Would never do.

But a paper marriage to save his beloved home was something he could do and do it willingly.

Logan selected a bottle of champagne from the wine fridge in the cellar next to the racks of vintage wine. His upcoming marriage to Layla might not be a real one in every sense of the word but it was surely worth celebrating their joint commitment to save Bellbrae.

Layla wheeled the serving trolley into the green dining room rather than risk carrying plates and dishes. Because of the muscle grafts performed to keep her leg functioning as best as it could, it was often weaker and more painful at the end of the day. And the last thing she wanted to do was make a fool of herself by losing her balance again and needing Logan's assistance. She was already feeling a little nervous about having dinner with him.

In the early days, Aunt Elsie had been very old-school about dining with the family upstairs and had always insisted Layla eat in the kitchen with her. But since the death of Logan's grandmother the rules had been relaxed as Angus McLaughlin had appreciated the company at dinner to get him through the long lonely evenings.

But she had never dined alone with Logan.

The green dining room was one Layla's favourite rooms in the castle. It had windows that overlooked the loch on the estate and the Highlands beyond. She left the curtains open as the moon had risen and was shining a bolt of shimmering silver across the crushed silk surface of the water.

Logan came back from the cellar just as Layla was straightening the settings on the table. He was carrying a bottle of French champagne in one hand and holding two crystal glasses by the stems in the other.

'I seem to recall you like champagne. But if you'd prefer wine…'

'No, I love champagne. It's my favourite drink.' She raised her brows when she saw the label. 'Gosh, that's a good one. But should we be wasting it on an everyday dinner?'

He placed the glasses on the table and began to remove the foil covering and wire from the cork. 'This isn't an everyday dinner. Tonight, we're celebrating our success in saving Bellbrae. That's worth ten thousand bottles of this drop.'

Layla watched as he deftly removed the cork and poured the champagne into the two crystal glasses. He handed her a glass and raised his own glass in a toast. 'To saving Bellbrae.'

She sipped the champagne, savouring the honey and lavender notes as they burst on her tongue. 'Mmm…lovely.'

Logan put his glass down and reached for something inside his trouser pocket. 'I have something for you.' He took out a vintage emerald-green velvet ring box and handed it to her.

Layla knew exactly what was inside the box. She'd helped Aunt Elsie pack away Logan's grandmother's things when Margaret McLaughlin had died from complications after routine surgery. The

collection of beautiful heirloom jewellery had fascinated Layla so much she had secretly looked at it
on many occasions when no one had been around.
She knew the code to the safe where it was kept,
and had even tried various pieces on, looking at
herself in the mirror, pretending she was a princess about to be married to the handsome prince
of her dreams.

Layla put her champagne glass down and prised
open the lid of the box and stared at the gorgeous
Art Deco setting with its array of glittering diamonds. 'Oh, my… I'd forgotten how beautiful
your grandmother's ring is.' She met his gaze. 'But
surely you don't want me to wear it? I mean, given
the circumstances of our…um…marriage?'

His expression was largely unreadable…all
except for the way his eyes dipped to her mouth
before going back to mesh with hers. 'My grandmother would want you to have it. She was fond
of you. Try it on. See if it fits. We can have it re-
sized if not.'

Layla already knew how well it fitted but
didn't want to reveal her guilty secret. She took
the ring out of the box, a part of her disappointed
he wasn't the one slipping it over her finger for
her, just as a man deeply in love with his fiancée
would do. But nothing about their engagement
was normal, so how silly of her to wish for things
she couldn't have.

But as if Logan had suddenly read her mind, he held out his palm for the ring. 'Here—let me do that. I believe it's my job.' There was a strange quality to his voice, a low deep chord of some un-identifiable emotion.

Layla placed the ring in the middle of his palm and held her breath as he took her hand in his. Her fingers were so white against the tan of his, her skin alive with sensations—tingly, fizzing sensations—that sent tiny zaps of electricity to the far reaches of her body.

He slid the ring over the knuckles of her ring finger and smiled when it met no resistance. 'It's like it was made for you.'

She was so captivated by his smile she forgot to look down at the ring on her finger. It had been years since she had seen him give a genuine smile. Not one of those half-baked twists of his mouth but a real smile that involved his eyes, making them crinkle attractively at the corners. He looked younger, less stressed, more approachable. The grief-damaged landscape of his face restored to one of hope instead of quiet despair. He was still holding her hand, his fingers warm and gentle as if he was holding a kitten.

The atmosphere changed as if there was a sud-den rent in time. A stillness. A silence waiting with bated breath for something to happen…

Layla couldn't tear her gaze away from his

mouth, couldn't stop wondering what it would be like to feel his lips against her own. She moistened her own lips with a darting movement of her tongue, her heart giving an extra beat like a musician misreading a musical score. 'I—I don't know what to say...'

'Don't say anything.' The pitch of his voice went down another notch and he slid his other hand under the curtain of her hair, his eyes locked on hers.

Every nerve tingled at his touch, every cell in her body throbbing with awareness. His eyes were the deepest blue she had ever seen them—bluer than the Bellbrae loch at midnight, bluer than a midnight winter sky. He was still holding her left hand, the heat from his hand seeping into her body with the potency of a powerful narcotic. She was aware of every part of his hand where it touched hers—the pads of his fingertips, the latent strength of his fingers, the protective warmth of his palm.

Layla forgot to breathe. She was transfixed by the slow descent of his mouth towards hers, spellbound by the clean fresh scent of his warm breath, mesmerised by the magnetic force drawing her inexorably closer, closer, closer to his lips. It was as if she had been waiting her entire life for this to happen. She hadn't been truly alive until now. She had been a formless ghost wandering through life until this moment when she had morphed into a live and vibrant female body with urgent needs and desires. Her heart sped up, her pulse leapt, her anticipation for the touchdown of his lips so acute it was almost unbearable.

Kiss me. Kiss me. Kiss me.

It was a silent chant keeping time with the pounding beat of her heart.

But suddenly Logan dropped his hold and stepped back, opening and closing his fingers as if to rid himself of the taint of touching her. 'Forgive me. That wasn't meant to happen.' His tone was brusque, his expression masked.

Layla was so overcome with disappointment she couldn't find her voice. She couldn't bear to look at his face in case she saw his disgust for her written on his features. The cruel taunts of her teenage boyfriend echoed out of the past in her head.

'You're ugly. You're a cripple. Who would ever want you?'

She looked down at her left hand where the ring was mockingly glinting, her stomach plummeting in despair. Such a beautiful ring for a girl who couldn't even attract a man enough for him to kiss her. What a mockery that ring was. A glittering, glaring, gut-wrenching reminder of everything Layla was not and never could be.

'It's okay,' she said at last, forcing herself to meet his gaze. 'I understand completely.'

He sucked in a deep breath, sending his hand

through his hair so roughly it left deep crooked finger trails. 'I don't think you do.'

Layla turned and got down to the business of serving their meal onto the plates where she had left them on the sideboard, next to the serving trolley. She placed the plates on the dining table and glanced his way. 'I think I do understand, Logan. This engagement is nothing like your last. You loved Susannah.' She released a painful breath. 'You still love her. That's why getting engaged to me makes you feel so uncomfortable, because you feel you're betraying her memory.'

A muscle in his jaw flickered as if he was grinding down on his molars. 'I don't wish to discuss Susannah with you or anyone.' His eyes were like closed windows. Curtains drawn. Shutters down.

Layla sat down at the table and spread her napkin over her lap. 'I realise you're still grieving. I'm sorry things have worked out the way they have— for her and for you. It was the saddest thing, especially since you've had so many other tragic losses in your life. But I think your grandfather was right in encouraging you to move on with your life.'

'Oh, so you quite like the way he went about it, do you?' His tone was as caustic as flesh-eating acid.

Layla pressed her lips together, fighting to control her see-sawing emotions. One second she was furious with him, the next she felt sad he couldn't let go of the past. 'Please sit down and have dinner. I'm getting a crick in my neck looking up at you.'

Logan strode over to the table and pulled out the chair and sat down, his knees bumping hers under the table. She shifted back a bit, trying to ignore the rush of heat that shot through her legs and straight to her core. Why couldn't she be immune to him? Why was she so acutely aware of him?

They began eating in a stiff silence, only the clanging discordant music of cutlery scraping against crockery puncturing the air.

Layla drank her glass of champagne and Logan refilled her glass as if he were a robotic waiter, but she noticed he didn't drink from his. His untouched cha.npagne glass stood in front of his place setting, releasing bubble after bubble in a series of tiny vertical towers.

She picked up her glass with her left hand and the diamonds on the ring winked at her under the chandelier light coming from overhead. Something was niggling at the back of her brain... Why hadn't Logan given Susannah his grandmother's ring? Layla remembered Susannah's engagement ring as being ultra-modern and flashy. It was a look-at-me ring that was not to Layla's taste at all. 'Logan?'

He looked up from the mechanical task of relaying food from his plate to his mouth. 'What?' His curt tone wasn't exactly encouraging, neither was the heavy frown between his eyes.

Layla toyed with the ring on her left hand. 'Why didn't you give your grandmother's ring to Susannah when you became engaged?'

Something passed through his gaze with camera shutter speed. 'She didn't like vintage jewellery.' He put his cutlery down and shifted his water glass an infinitesimal distance. 'I didn't take it personally. I was happy to buy her what she wanted.' He picked up his cutlery again and stabbed a piece of parsnip as if it had personally offended him.

Layla waited until he had finished his mouthful before asking, 'How are her parents and siblings coping? Do you hear from them or contact them yourself?'

A shadow moved across his face like clouds scudding across a troubled autumn sky. 'I used to call them or drop in on them in the early days but not lately. It only upset them to be reminded.' He put his cutlery down in the finished position on his plate and rested his arms on the table, his frown a roadmap of lines.

Layla reached for his forearm and gave it a gentle squeeze. 'I can only imagine how awful it must have been to have come home and found her… like that…'

He pulled his arm away and sat stiffly upright in his chair, his expression as blank as the white tablecloth. But after a long moment he relaxed his posture as if something tightly bound within him had loosened slightly. 'When someone takes their own life it's not like any other death.' His gaze was haunted, his tone bleak. 'The guilt, the what-ifs, the if-onlys, the what-could-I-have-done-to-prevent-this are unbearable.' He expelled a heavy breath and continued, 'I blame myself for not seeing the signs.'

'You mustn't blame yourself but I understand how you and most people do,' Layla said. 'But I read somewhere that sixteen percent of suicides are completely unheralded. It's a snap in the moment decision borne out of some hidden anguish.'

Logan picked up his champagne and drained it in a couple of swallows, placing the glass back down with a savage little thump. 'There were signs but I ignored them.' He waited a beat or two before continuing in a ragged voice. 'She had an eating disorder. Bulimia. I don't know how I missed it.' His mouth twisted in a grimace and his tone became tortured with self-loathing. 'How can you live with someone for months and not know that about her?'

Layla reached for his hand but this time he didn't pull away. 'Shame makes people hide lots of stuff. Bulimia is mostly a secret disease and much harder to pick up on than anorexia, where the physical effect is so obvious.'

Logan looked down at their joined hands and turned his over to anchor hers to the table. He began to absently stroke the back of her hand with his thumb, the caress only light, lazy almost, but no less magical. Nerves she hadn't known she possessed reacted as if touched by a live electrode, zinging, singing, tingling.

He lifted his gaze to hers and something toppled over in her stomach. His thumb stilled on the back of her hand but he didn't release her. His gaze moved over her face as if he were memorising her features one by one. When he got to her mouth she couldn't stop herself from sweeping the tip of her tongue across her lips—it was an impulse she had zero control over.

Logan gave her hand another quick squeeze in time with the on-off movement of his lips, in a blink-and-you'd-miss-it smile. A smile that didn't reach high enough to take the shadows out of his eyes. But then he let go of her hand and sat back in his chair and picked up his water glass and drained it, placing it back down with a definitive thud.

'Finish your dinner. We have a busy day tomorrow meeting with the lawyer to organise the legal paperwork. Rather than drive, I've taken the liberty of organising a flight from Inverness to Edinburgh.' His business-like tone and abrupt change of subject was disquieting and left her with far too many questions unanswered.

'Okay…' Layla wanted to know more about his relationship with Susannah. She had idolised them as a couple, seeing them as a match made in heaven. Feeling jealous of the love they'd shared, hoping one day someone would love her in the same way. But finding out their relationship might not have been as open and wonderful as she had imagined made her understand why Logan was so reluctant to commit to anyone else.

But Layla had personal experience of the tricky question of how well could you know anyone, even someone you had lived with for years. Didn't her childhood circumstances prove that? Her father had always been a difficult man; prone to angry outbursts, regular violence—especially when on drugs or drunk, but who would have thought he was capable of the crime he'd eventually committed— driving into a tree at full speed to kill the family he'd purported to love?

'The legal stuff…' She chewed her lip for a moment, desperate to get her mind off the accident that had killed her mother and changed her own life for ever. 'You mean a pre-nup, right?'

'Pre-nups are commonplace these days. Please don't be offended by my desire for one. You have your own assets to consider—your cleaning business, for example.'

Layla gave a self-deprecating snort and picked up her champagne glass. 'Yeah, right. My assets hardly compare to yours. You have offices all over the UK and Europe. My office is basically on my phone. I decided to give up my Edinburgh office after your grandfather died to come back and help Aunt Elsie. It seemed easier to work from here until everything is settled with the estate.'

'I'm sorry you've been so inconvenienced,' he said, looking at her with a concerned frown. 'I had no idea you'd given up your office.'

She waved a dismissive hand. 'I was glad to come home. Flossie was missing your grandfather and Aunt Elsie was finding it hard to do everything on her own.'

'Your business is doing well, though, isn't it? You're running at a decent profit?'

Layla was not going to admit to him or to anyone how close to the wind she sailed at times with her business. Failure was not an option. A nightmare that haunted her, yes, but *not* an option. Failure would prove she was nothing but a product of her chaotic childhood—a child of addicts. Her parents had had no ambition beyond the goal of sourcing enough alcohol and drugs for their next binge.

Owning her own cleaning business gave Layla power and control, and God alone knew how little of that she'd had in her childhood. 'I do okay.' She put her glass back down again.

'How okay?' His gaze was as direct as a laser pointer.

Layla shifted in her seat and lowered her eyes to the remains of her meal on her plate. 'It's not always easy to get reliable workers. It takes time to build up trust, to know they're always going to do the right thing by me and the people I get them to clean for.' She met his gaze and continued. 'They're cleaning people's homes where valuables and personal effects are not always under lock and key, and often the clients are not at home when my staff are there.'

A frown brought his ink-black eyebrows together. 'Don't you do background checks on them first?'

'Some of the young people I employ wouldn't pass a background check,' Layla said. 'They need someone to give them a break for once. To not always be expecting them to slip up or fail. I believe in showing trust first and teaching them some skills, hoping it triggers the desire in them to make better choices.' The sort of choices she wished her parents had made.

'Admirable of you, but you're setting yourself up for guaranteed disappointment.' His tone matched his cynical expression.

Layla hoisted her chin a fraction. 'My vision for my business is not just about making a big profit. It's about making a difference in people's lives. Lives that others have judged and found wanting. But I know how powerful it can be when someone believes in you. Someone who sees something in you that no one else does. It's…it's transformative.'

His eyes moved over her face like a search-light for a long moment and she had to fight not to shift her gaze.

'Is that because of what happened in your child-hood?' His tone had lost its cynical edge. 'My grandparents giving permission for you to come and live here with your great-aunt?'

'It's getting late.' Layla pushed back her chair and rose from the table and began to gather the plates. Next he'd be asking her to spill all about her miserable childhood and that she was determined *not* to do. Thankfully, privacy laws had prevented the McLaughlins from hearing too many of the gory details about her early years—details Layla dearly wished she could forget. 'I think I can hear Flossie asking to be let out.'

Logan placed a hand over her forearm as she reached for his plate. 'I don't want you to wait on me, Layla. I want you to talk to me. There's a lot we don't know about each other, and we need to know it if we're going to make our relationship appear genuine.'

She glanced at his hand on her arm and gave him a pointed look. 'Do you mind?'

He released her hand, his tone and expression softening. 'I don't know all the details but I know your background was difficult. It must have been, otherwise you wouldn't have ended up living here. I think it's great how you've taken charge and started your own business. But don't be too proud to ask for help if you need it.' He rose to his feet and pushed in his chair, adding, 'There's one other thing I think I should tell you. We'll have to get married abroad and soon. According to Scottish law, there's a twenty-eight-day waiting period before we can get a marriage licence, and I don't want to lose any more valuable time.'

'Married abroad?' Layla opened and closed her mouth. 'Please tell me you're not thinking Vegas and an Elvis impersonator?'

He gave a crooked smile that made something in her chest ping like a latch springing open. 'No. But if you're not keen on an impersonal register office, how about a small and simple ceremony on a beach in Hawaii?'

Hawaii. The land of bikinis and beaches and beautiful bodies.

Oh, joy.

CHAPTER FOUR

A COUPLE OF days after the legal work was completed in Edinburgh, Layla flew business class with Logan to the island of Maui in Hawaii. The luxury villa he'd organised for their short stay was situated at Kapalua Bay beach, a gorgeous crescent of blindingly white sand and turquoise water and palm trees. Layla felt as if she was living in a dream sequence—swept away to an exotic location by a handsome billionaire who was intent on marrying her as quickly as he could.

But not for the romantic reasons her girlhood dreams had envisaged.

The speed and efficiency with which Logan set about achieving a goal was nothing less than breathtaking. Layla barely had time to get her head around the idea of a beach wedding, let alone buy the appropriate attire for it, when she found herself standing on the balcony of the beautiful villa overlooking the ocean with just minutes to spare before the ceremony.

Her wedding day.

It was strange to think that this time last week she had been a single woman with a simple goal of keeping her business on track. Now she was about to be married to a man she had known for most of her life who didn't love her the way a husband should love his bride.

But Logan did love his family's home and so did she, so it would have to be a good enough reason to marry. The *only* reason to marry, because the last thing she needed was to get silly ideas in her head about their relationship lasting beyond the year, as set down in the document his lawyer had drawn up.

One year and one year only.

The money Logan had transferred to her account on signing the document would guarantee Layla's business success. It was exactly the windfall she needed to expand her business from a scribbled sticky-note vision into a profit-making reality.

Logan came out to the balcony where she was standing looking at the view. She turned to face him with an attempt at a smile. Their wedding ceremony was minutes away but if he was uncomfortable or uneasy about what they were about to do, he wasn't showing it on his face. They might as well have been heading down the beach for an afternoon stroll.

He pushed back his shirt sleeve to glance at the silver watch on his strong tanned wrist. 'The celebrant will be here in ten minutes.'

'Okay...' Layla took a deep breath and smoothed her hand down over her churning stomach. 'Isn't it meant to be bad luck for you to see me in my dress before the ceremony?'

His eyes ran over the Bohemian-style white dress she had bought in a boutique in Edinburgh. It was enough like a wedding dress for her to feel like a bride, even if she wasn't a real one, and long enough to cover the scars on her leg. And—even more important—she could wear flat sandals or bare feet rather than struggle with heels.

'I can safely say I've already had more than my fair share of bad luck. You too, I imagine.' His tone was wry. 'You look beautiful, by the way.' His gaze held hers in a lock that did strange things to her insides. Tingling things, thrilling things. Forbidden things.

Layla was the first to look away, worried he would see things she didn't want him to see. Things she didn't even want to admit to herself. 'I don't have a bouquet or anything. I hope that's not bad luck too.'

He walked over to a box that was sitting on the coffee table in the large open-plan room off the balcony. She hadn't noticed it earlier as she'd been preoccupied with getting ready so soon after their arrival. Or it had been delivered while she was in the shower. He took the lid off and the sweet tropical scent of frangipanis filled the air. He took out a simple but beautiful bouquet and handed it to her.

'I hope this will do?'

'It's perfect.' Layla took the bouquet from him and bent her face to the creamy blooms with their egg-yolk-yellow hearts, the glorious fragrance drugging her senses. Not to mention Logan's intoxicating closeness doing exactly the same thing. He was dressed in an open-necked white shirt and mid-blue jacket and trousers that brought out the intense blue in his eyes and the deep olive tan of his skin. She could smell his aftershave—could even pick up the clean fruity smell of his shampoo from his recent shower. His jaw was freshly shaven and her fingers itched to touch his face to trace where the razor had glided over his tanned skin. She was aware of every inch of his body standing within touching distance of hers. Aware of every breath he took, every flare of his nostrils, every rustle of his clothes when he moved.

Within a few minutes they would be husband and wife.

On paper.

She had to keep reminding herself of that pesky little detail.

Logan held out his hand, his expression inscrutable. 'Ready to head down?'

Layla put her hand in his, holding the bouquet in the other, her heart thumping, her pulse racing. 'I'm ready.'

I think…

When they got down to the beach, Layla took off her sandals and Logan his shoes so they could walk on the sand. They walked together towards the celebrant, who was waiting for them on the beach with two witnesses—a couple, Makani and Ken, whose award-winning landscape design Logan had done for them at their main home in the Hamptons in the US a few years ago. They spent part of the year on Maui, where Makani had family. Logan had informed Layla earlier that he had told Makani and Ken nothing about the reason behind his sudden marriage to Layla, allowing them to draw the conclusion it was a genuine love match.

If only it was…

Then Layla wouldn't be feeling so conflicted about making promises that were essentially meaningless. Entering a marriage that after a year would be terminated.

The rhythm of the ocean lapping the shore was the only music to accompany them to their position in front of the male celebrant, who was holding two colourful leis. He gave the traditional Hawaiian welcome, placed the leis over their heads and began the simple service. 'We are gathered here today to join this man and this woman in marriage…'

Layla repeated the vows as instructed, intensely aware of Logan's warm blue gaze and the feel of his hand holding hers as he slid the wedding ring home on her finger. His voice as he said his vows was strong and steady and assured—no one would ever think he didn't mean a word he'd said. Apart from her, that is. But it was an act and good actors, the best actors, made themselves *feel* the emotion so they could bring authenticity to the scene.

'You may kiss the bride.'

Layla had fooled herself that Logan might skip this part of the service, especially since he had pulled away from kissing her the other day. But as soon as the celebrant spoke the words, Logan drew her closer and his head came down, down, down until his lips touched hers. She was expecting him to lift them straight off, to be satisfied with a perfunctory kiss for the sake of appearances, but the pressure of his lips changed, warmed, heated, hardened. Burned and branded.

Her lips moved with the sensual rhythm of his, opening to his, welcoming the slow sexy stroke of his tongue meeting hers for the first time. It wasn't a deep kiss—no tangling or thrusting of tongues—but gentle nudges and playful touches of lips and tongue tips that sent a shiver coursing through her body from the top of her sun-warmed head to the soles of her sand-caressed bare feet. There was a swooping sensation deep in her belly, an ache spreading in a river of heat, simmering, smouldering, sizzling in her core.

His lips were gentle and yet firm, purposeful, passionate and utterly addictive. Layla nudged his lips with her own, sweeping the tip of her tongue over his lower lip, delighting in the way his breath hitched and his hold on her tightened.

His hand glided down to the base of her spine, drawing her closer to the hard ridge of his stirring arousal. It was both shocking and exhilarating to feel the intimate pulse of his blood. Shocking, because she hadn't dared hope he would be attracted to her in such a way.

Layla slid her hands to the hard plane of his chest, feeling the thumpity-thump, thump-thump of his heart beneath her palm. She forgot about everything but the sensation of his lips moving with such exquisite expertise on hers, drawing from her a passionate response, a clawing and desperate need building in her body with such force it was overwhelming. Every nerve in her body seemed to be attuned to his mouth, to the warmth and potency of it, to the eroticism it boldly, blatantly promised.

She was so consumed by his kiss she no longer heard the swish and slap and sigh of the waves as they lapped and sucked at the shore. No longer aware of the ocean breeze stirring the fronds on the palm trees, no longer aware of the fine grains of sand beneath her feet or the sun shining down on her head.

The sound of the witnesses clapping seemed to snap Logan out of the moment. He lifted his mouth off hers and gave a crooked smile that said everything and yet nothing.

Layla licked her lips and tasted him, wanted him with a deep ache that vibrated in her core like a plucked cello string. Her heart was still racing, her pulse off the charts, her legs trembling. Now, *that* was a kiss. She felt dazed, stunned, spinning with lingering sensations. Her mouth still felt sensitive, her lips slightly swollen. She searched his gaze for any sign he was as affected by their kiss as she was but his gaze was like the ocean beside them with its mysterious depths and shifting shadows.

They were soon swept up in the hearty congratulations of Makani and Ken, followed by the official signing of the register. Logan had organised refreshments back at the villa but things had to be cut short when Makani got a call from her mother, who was babysitting their children, that the youngest was running a temperature.

'Sorry to leave so soon,' Makani said, and added with a twinkling smile, 'But just you wait until you have kids. Life will never be the same, but in a totally good way.'

'Now, now, honey,' Ken said, looping an arm around his wife's waist. 'Don't go putting baby ideas in their heads just yet. Let them enjoy their honeymoon.'

Honeymoon.

The word was enough to send another shiver shooting through Layla's body.

Logan saw his guests out and came back to where Layla was sipping a glass of champagne on one of the sofas overlooking the ocean view. If he closed his eyes, he could take himself back to the moment of their kiss at the ceremony. Damn it—he didn't even need to close his eyes. He could still taste the milk and honey sweetness of her mouth—could still feel the thrum of lust deep in his body.

He was relieved he was good at concealing his emotions because that kiss had rocked him to the core. He hadn't wanted it to end. He had lost track of where they were and why they were there. All he'd cared about, all he'd craved was the smooth, soft, sweet delicacy of her mouth moving against his. The shy playfulness of her tongue had sent a rocket blast of need to his groin. Triggering a need that was still humming in the background—a low, persistent hum he was doing his level best to ignore.

Their marriage was on paper. That was the deal. It was for one year and one year only and then it would be over.

No damage done.

But that kiss had already done damage because he wanted to kiss her again. Their kiss had made him think about taking things further, doing things he had no business doing with her. Things he had no business doing with anyone. He didn't do long-term intimate relationships.

Not again.

But that kiss had stirred something inside him— something that until now had been lying dormant, in a coma, dead. The touch of Layla's pillow-soft lips had sent electrodes of awareness to every part of his body, jolting it awake, making his flesh hungry, greedy for sensual satiation. Not for the quick-fix, hook-up type sex he had indulged in during the last seven years. He would be fooling himself if he said he had enjoyed those encounters beyond the brief physical relief they had provided.

But he suspected making love with Layla would be entirely different, which was why he couldn't allow himself to go there. Couldn't allow himself permission to even *think* about the possibility. There would be too many complications when it came to ending their arrangement. The sort of complications he could well do without.

Layla turned her head to look at him, still cradling her champagne, her expression bland. 'So, here we are, then.'

Logan fought to keep a frown off his face and

tried a crooked smile instead but wasn't sure it was too convincing. 'Yes…' He picked up the bottle of champagne in the ice bucket and brought it over to where she was sitting to refill her glass. 'More?'

She placed her hand over the top of the glass. 'Better not. I might start saying things I wouldn't normally say.' She gave a twisted smile and added, '*In vino veritas* and all that.'

'In the wine lies the truth.' Logan grunted in agreement, topping up his own glass, and then put the champagne bottle back in the ice bucket with a rattle against the ice cubes and continued, 'Drunk words, sober thoughts.' He wondered what she would say if he told her what he was thinking. What he'd been thinking ever since he'd kissed her. No, even before that—when he'd encountered her in the north tower at Bellbrae. Something had happened, something had changed between them and he wasn't sure how to change it back.

There was a beat or two of silence.

Logan turned back to look at her. 'Feel free to speak your mind with me, Layla. I don't expect you to have to drink to excess in order to do it.'

She leaned forward to put her glass on the coffee table, her eyes slipping out of reach of his. She sat back and smoothed a crease out of her dress before returning her gaze to his with disquieting intensity. 'Why did you kiss me like that at the ceremony?'

Logan took a sip of his champagne before responding. Not because he needed alcohol but because he didn't know how to answer without betraying himself. He wanted to kiss her again. Now. And not just kiss her but explore her beautiful body with the same thoroughness. He wanted to run his hands through the silk cloud of her hair. He wanted to kiss the soft creamy skin at the base of her throat, to trail his tongue along the contours of her collarbones, to breathe in the flowery scent of her until he was drunk with it.

'It seemed the right thing to do at the time.' Logan's tone held no trace of the battle going on inside him. 'Malaki and Ken, and indeed the celebrant, would have thought it strange if we hadn't kissed.'

A tiny frown wrinkled her brow. 'True. But you kissed me as if you didn't want to stop.' Her teeth snagged her bottom lip and she added, 'Was that… just acting?' Her voice had a note of uncertainty that was strangely touching.

Logan put his champagne glass down and released a long breath. 'No. It wasn't just acting.' He closed his eyes in a slow blink and dragged a hand down his face. 'It was a moment of foolishness that won't be repeated.'

Must not be repeated. Must not. Must not. Must not. He drummed it into his head but his body was offline. Off-script.

There was a silence broken only by the sound of waves pulsing against the shore.

Layla rose from the sofa and wandered over to look out of the open balcony doors to the beach below. Her arms were around her mid-section, her posture stiff and guarded as if she was shielding herself from an expected insult. 'So, you didn't enjoy it, then?' Her voice still echoed with self-doubt.

Logan told himself to stay where he was—to keep his distance. To not tempt himself beyond his endurance by crossing the floor to her. But step by step he went, programmed by a force he had no way of countering. He placed his hands on the tops of her shoulders, turning her to face him. Her grey-green gaze assiduously avoided his so he tipped up her chin with one of his fingers so she had no choice but to meet his eyes. 'I enjoyed it way too much and therein lies our problem.'

She moistened her lips with the tip of her tongue, making them even more unbearably tempting. 'Why is that a problem?' Her voice was as low and husky as a whispered secret and it sent shivers racing down his spine.

Logan stroked his thumb across her cheek, marvelling at the creamy softness of her skin. 'You know why.' His tone was so low and rough it sounded like he'd been filing his tonsils with a blacksmith's rasp.

'Because of our paper marriage?' Her eyes reminded him of cloudy sea glass.

He couldn't seem to stop his thumb from stroking her cheek, couldn't stop his gaze from drinking in every nuance of her features. Couldn't stop the thrum of lust that assailed his body like an invisible invader. Marching through every inch of his flesh, aching, wanting, needing. 'We have to be sensible about this, Layla.'

I have to be sensible. I have to be in control.

She reached up with her hand and stroked his jaw from his cheekbone to his chin, her eyes luminous. 'I think I must have already had too much champagne because right now I want you to kiss me again. I want to know if the first time was a fluke or…or something else.'

It was the 'something else' that most worried Logan. He fought every aroused cell in his body but it was a battle he was worried he might not win, or at least not in the long run. One year of this level of temptation and he would be a certifiable mess. How much temptation could a man endure? Especially for a man who had actively avoided contact as intimate as this.

Kissing a hook-up date was one thing, kissing someone he had known for years and was currently married to was another. Their paper marriage would be incinerated, obliterated if he gave in to the temptation to kiss her again. One taste of her mouth had already unleashed something feral inside him, something he wasn't sure he could control for too much longer.

Calling on every bit of willpower he possessed, Logan dropped his hand from her face and took a step back. 'I'm sorry, Layla, but this can't happen. I made the rules for a reason.'

Her gaze reminded him of the still surface of a lake. Calm. Controlled. But there was a faint ripple of disappointment around the edges. 'Okeydokey.' Her words and tone were flippant given the topic under discussion. So too her overly bright, breezy smile. 'We'll leave it at that, then.' She moved across the room to where the champagne bottle was and topped up her glass. She turned and held her glass up in a toast, her expression faintly mocking. 'Long live the rules.'

Logan ground his teeth so hard he mentally apologised to his dentist. 'Listen—I'm not doing this to insult you. It's not personal.'

'Isn't it?' Her eyes were glittering as brightly as the diamonds on her left hand next to her wedding ring. Not glittering with tears but with anger.

He let out a slowly controlled breath, anchoring his hands on his hips like he was about to deliver an important lecture. Which he was, but he suspected he was the one who needed to hear it most. 'Think about it. If we were to have a normal relationship, it would be much more complicated to end it when the year was up. This way we can get an annulment and leave it at that. No harm done.' He dropped his hands from his hips. 'I'm not saying it will be an easy year. But we're both mature adults, and I want us to remain friends at the end of it.'

She rolled her lips together, her arms crossed, with her champagne glass tilted at a threatening-to-spill angle. 'What have you told your brother about us? Does he know it's just a paper marriage?'

Logan folded back the cuffs of his shirt for something to do with his hands. 'I haven't spoken to him yet. He hasn't answered any of my calls or texts or emails.' Which, unfortunately, wasn't unusual when Robbie was on one of his gambling sprees.

'But what will you tell him?'

It was a question Logan had been asking himself for the last few days. He hadn't been able to contact his younger brother to talk about anything, much less his sudden marriage to Layla Campbell, the housekeeper's great-niece. 'He will have seen the will by now but I'm hoping he'll accept our marriage as the real deal. It's not as if you and I are complete strangers and he knows my grandfather always had a soft spot for you.'

'It might be tricky convincing Robbie we're a genuine couple when he comes home to Bellbrae sometime. You know what he's like—he often arrives unannounced. If we're sleeping on opposite sides of the castle it will look kind of odd.'

Logan could see her point. His brother might be immature and reckless but he wasn't a total fool. It wouldn't take Robbie long to pick up on any irregularities in Logan's relationship with Layla, and their living arrangements in particular. 'We could move into the west tower. The large suite that has the connecting bedrooms.' He would be far closer to her than he'd intended—sleeping with just a door between them.

A door he would keep locked—literally and mentally.

'Fine,' Layla said, draining her glass. 'But can I make a request?'

'Sure.'

She put her glass down and faced him squarely. 'When we're pretending to be happily married to Robbie and anyone else, will you use terms of endearment or just call me Layla?'

'What would you prefer?'

'You can call me anything but babe.' She gave a faint shudder as if even saying the word upset her.

'Why not babe?'

A hard light came into her eyes and her expression set like fast-acting glue. 'Someone I used to know used it a lot. I've loathed it ever since.'

Before Logan could ask her to elaborate, she turned and walked out of the room, leaving him with just the lingering fragrance of her perfume.

CHAPTER FIVE

ARGH! WHY HAD she drunk that second glass of champagne? Their beach wedding had got to her, that was why. She had been swept away by the romantic setting, swept away by Logan's kiss. The kiss that had sent shivers up and down her spine and driven silly ideas into her head. Ideas of him wanting things to go further, him wanting *her*. Not just physically but intellectually and emotionally.

But he had drawn a line in the sand. *Do Not Cross*.

Layla plonked herself down on the bed in her room with a despondent sigh. She'd made a class-A fool of herself, practically begging Logan to kiss her. Shame washed through her at how gauche she had been—how unworldly and foolish to think he might want to tweak the rules on their relationship.

But his kiss had been so...so genuine. So authentic. So powerfully passionate she could feel it on her lips even now. She only had to close her eyes and she was back there on the warm grainy sand, with the waves washing against the shore with their fringe of white lace, and Logan's mouth clamped to hers as if he never wanted to let her go. The need he had stirred in her was still humming in her body—a faint background ache she couldn't ignore.

Layla hitched up the hem of her dress and wriggled her feet and curled her toes. The white jagged scars on her left leg a jarring reminder of her past. The past that contained memories she wished she could forget. Painful memories that were embedded so deeply into her brain she still had nightmares.

Babe. The word she loathed because her father had used it to address her mother in love and hate and everything in between. The word her father had said in the moments before the car had slammed into the tree.

Layla pushed herself off the bed and walked over to the windows overlooking the beach. She hugged her arms around her body, trying to contain the disturbing images that flashed into her brain every time she thought of the accident. Accident? What a misnomer that was. It had been no accident. Her father had wanted to kill them all and had just about succeeded in doing so. He and her mother had died at the scene but Layla had been saved by a passing motorist—an off-duty nurse who had controlled the bleeding until the paramedics had arrived. *Lucky Layla*. That was what she'd heard the medical staff call her at the hospital.

Why, then, didn't she feel it?

Layla blinked away the past and focussed on the beach below. The turquoise water beckoned but she hadn't swum since rehab after the accident. And you could hardly call *that* swimming. She wasn't sure she could even do it anymore. And she couldn't imagine doing it without a body suit on, because going out in public with her scars on show drew too many stares, too many pitying looks, too many intrusive questions.

But on a whim she still couldn't explain, she had bought a swimsuit when she'd bought her wedding dress. It was a strapless emerald-green one-piece with a ruched panel in the front and a matching sarong. It was still in her suitcase—she hadn't bothered unpacking it—because taking it out would be admitting she longed to swim, to feel the cool caress of ocean around her body, to be lifted weightless in its embrace. Free to move with perfect symmetry instead of her syncopated gait.

Layla narrowed her gaze when she saw a tall figure walking to the water. Logan had changed into a black hipster swimming costume, which showcased his athletic physique to perfection. Lean and taut with well-trained muscles, his skin tanned from numerous trips abroad, he turned every female head on the beach but seemed completely unaware of it. He waded through the waves until he got to deeper water and began striking out beyond the breakers in an effortless freestyle that was both graceful and powerful.

She turned away from the window with another sigh. She was on beautiful Maui in Hawaii with her brand-new husband who didn't want her other than as a means to an end.

Where was Lucky Layla now?

Logan towelled off on the beach after his swim, but the restlessness in him hadn't gone away in spite of the punishing exercise. He'd considered asking Layla to join him for a swim but had decided against it. This was not a honeymoon. They didn't have to spend every minute of the day together— even if he wanted to a lot more than he should.

He walked back to the villa and found Layla sitting on one of the sun lounge chairs on the terrace overlooking the beach. She was wearing blue denim jeans and ballet flats and an untucked white cotton shirt. Her head was shaded by a wide-brimmed hat and her eyes screened behind a pair of sunglasses. She looked up from the magazine she was flicking through and lowered her sunglasses a fraction to look at him. 'How was the water?'

'Wet.'

She pushed her sunglasses back up to the bridge of her nose. 'Funny, ha-ha.'

Logan took the sun lounge seat beside hers and hooked one arm around one of his bent knees. 'Did you bring a swimming costume with you?'

'Yes, but I don't want to swim.' Her tone was brusque to the point of rudeness, her gaze staring out in front of her rather than facing him. 'Please don't ask me again.'

'If you're worried about your leg, then let me assure you—'

Her gaze whipped around to his with such speed it dislodged her hat and she had to steady it with one of her hands. 'You laid down some rules so I'm going to do the same. I don't like swimming. I don't like wearing bikinis or shorts or skirts that are above the knee. And if you *do* want me to wear them, then you've married the wrong person.' She removed her hand from holding her hat in place and turned back to stare out at the ocean.

Logan swung his legs over the side of the sun lounge seat and leaned his arms on his knees, studying her rigid features. Her mouth was set, her chin at a haughty height, her eyes fixed on a view he could tell she wasn't even registering.

'Layla.' He kept his voice low and gentle. 'Look at me.'

Her fingers began to pick at a frayed patch on her jeans, her mouth still set in a stubborn line.

'I know what you're going to say, so don't bother saying it.'

'Tell me what you think I'm going to say.'

She pulled a thread out of the patch on her jeans and played tug-of-war with a series of sharp little tugs until it snapped. 'You're going to tell me I'm being silly about being self-conscious about my leg. That I should try and live a normal life and not care what anyone says or if they stare and ask rude questions.' She rolled the broken pieces of thread into a ball and dropped them onto the table beside her chair. 'But you're you. You're not me.'

Logan took one of her hands and anchored it against his thigh close to his bent knee. 'You're not silly to be self-conscious. It's tough having anything that draws unwelcome attention. But it concerns me you're limiting your enjoyment of life because of other people's reaction or judgement.'

She went to pull her hand out from under his but he countered it with a little more pressure. Her palm was soft against his thigh—warm and soft— and he couldn't stop imagining how it would feel on other parts of his body. His groin stirred, his blood rushed, his self-control went AWOL. Before he could stop himself, he brought her hand up to his mouth, pressing a light kiss to her bent knuckles. She gave a little whole-body shiver as if his touch was having the same effect on her as hers was on him. The tip of her tongue darted out to sweep a layer of moisture over her lips, her throat rising and falling in an audible swallow.

He took her sunglasses off her nose and laid them aside so he could mesh his gaze with hers. 'You don't have to be self-conscious around me. If we're going to convince Robbie and others that this is the real deal, then we're both going to have to feel more relaxed around each other. And even if we don't feel it we'll have to act it.'

Her pupils were like black ink spots, her eyelashes miniature fans. Her gaze dipped to his mouth, her indrawn breath sounding ragged. 'Relaxed…in what way?'

Logan turned her hand over and stroked his thumb over her palm in a rhythmic fashion. 'There will be occasions when we'll be required to show some affection. Holding hands, a kiss on the cheek or a quick peck on the lips for appearances' sake. It would look odd if we didn't.'

'Okay…' Her voice was as soft as the whisper of the afternoon breeze. 'But earlier today you were pretty determined we weren't going to kiss again.'

'Unless absolutely necessary.'

Her eyebrows lifted in a wry manner. 'And who gets to decide whether it's necessary or not?'

'Me.' Logan released her hand and stood. He was unapologetic for being so adamant. He wanted no blurry boundaries. He wanted control at all times. He wanted to keep his wanting under lock and key.

She anchored her hat and tilted her head to look up at him. 'Is that fair?'

'Probably not but that's the way it's going to be.' He scooped up his towel and flung it around his shoulders. 'I'm heading in for a shower. I've booked a restaurant for dinner at eight. It's a short walk from here but we can get a taxi if you'd prefer.'

Pride shone in her eyes and rang in her voice. 'That won't be necessary.'

Layla dressed for dinner later that evening with her mind still replaying their conversation out on the terrace. When he'd come to join her still dressed in nothing but his close-fitting swimming briefs, she had almost fainted on the spot with lust. And when he'd placed her hand on his bare thigh, it had been all she could do not to move it up higher. Her hand had tingled the whole time he'd held it.

When he'd repeatedly stroked his thumb across her palm, a fluttery sensation had gone through her belly and her female hormones went crazy. They were still going crazy. Her body was awake to needs it hadn't been conscious of before. Needs that made her long to have his hands stroking other places on her body. Places where no one had ever touched her.

Layla smoothed down the black all-in-one, spaghetti-strapped pantsuit that clung to her slim frame and widened at the legs in an elegant flare. It was a shame she couldn't wear high heels but the small kitten-heeled shoes were about as glamourous as she was prepared to go. She had lived her life since the car crash living safely and she didn't want to change. *Couldn't* change when it came to it. She had spent months and months in hospital and then more in a rehabilitation clinic. Long lonely bewildering months trying to get used to her new circumstances.

Adjusting to the presence of a new friend—survivor guilt.

Feeling guilty about her pretence of grieving for the loss of her parents, when what she had really felt was relief. She had felt far more relief over not losing her leg than grief over losing her parents. What did that say about her? Her scars reminded her every day of the conflict of her emotions. To this day, she felt relieved to be finally free of the chaotic family life both her parents had been responsible for, although she held her father to most of the blame.

A crazy, unpredictable life where alcohol and drugs had been on the table instead of food. A life where violence and shouting insults and smashing plates and glasses had been commonplace. Where there had been no peace even when it was quiet because you knew there was a storm brewing that could erupt at any moment. Without warning. Without any recognisable trigger. It just happened and you had to take shelter if you could and pray like crazy if you couldn't.

Layla sighed and swept her hair up in a make-shift bun, blocking her thoughts of the past like a shutter coming down. She refused to be a victim these days. She was strong and resilient and was fiercely proud of what she had achieved so far. And this temporary marriage with Logan would help her achieve even more. The money he had deposited into her bank account had already turned her financial situation around. Her business expansion plans could go ahead without fear of failure. She would focus on the positives of their marriage arrangement, not the niggling negatives.

She opened her cosmetics bag and touched up her make-up, spritzing perfume on her pulse points and applying lip-gloss to her lips. She gave herself a quick appraisal by turning this way and that in front of the mirror, deciding that even if she wasn't perfect, at least she was passable.

Logan had just ended a call dealing with a work issue on a large project he had going on in Tuscany when Layla came into the sitting room. Her all-in-one black outfit skimmed her slim figure in all the right places. Places he couldn't stop thinking about touching, caressing, exploring. Her make-up highlighted the regal elegance of her finely drawn features—the smoky eyeshadow and mascara on her lashes making her eyes stand out. Her chestnut hair was on top of her head in a loosely casual knot, leaving her swan-like neck and creamy shoulders exposed.

He imagined kissing a trail of light kisses along her smooth skin, down to her collarbones, down to the slight swell of her breasts. He imagined himself unclipping her hair from its knot and running his fingers through it to see if it was as silky as it looked. Her lips were shimmering with a layer of pink-toned lip-gloss and all he could think about was pressing his lips to hers to remove it with a kiss. He could still recall the sweet vanilla and honey taste of her mouth, could still feel the texture of her lips—soft…impossibly soft and responsive. Could still feel the background beat of desire ticking in his blood.

Oh, boy, he had some work to do on his willpower. Some big work.

If he was fantasising like this on day one of their marriage, what would he be like at the end of it?

'You look beautiful,' he said, slipping his phone into his trouser pocket.

A light tinge of pink pooled high in her cheeks and she lowered her gaze a fraction. 'Thank you.'

'Shall we go?' Logan led the way outside so

they could walk to the restaurant, which was only a short stroll further along the bay. The night air had a salty tang from the ocean and there was a gibbous moon. Layla walked beside him in silence but he was increasingly aware of her limp. She was wearing small heels but they clearly weren't giving her the stability she needed. After she gave a precarious wobble, he reached for her hand and enveloped it in his. 'The pathway is a little uneven here.'

She glanced up at him with a brief smile of thanks and looked away again. They walked the rest of the way in silence but Logan was aware of every whorl of her skin where it touched his. Aware of the light flowery fragrance she was wearing, aware of how her head only came to just below his shoulders.

They came to the restaurant and were soon led to their table overlooking Kapalua Bay. The waiter took their drinks orders and left them with menus. Logan gave the menu a cursory glance because he could barely take his eyes off Layla. He had never spent so much concentrated time with her before. But when it came to that, he hadn't spent much time with anyone over the last seven years. He had preferred to be alone with his thoughts, with his regrets, with his guilt. Not just his guilt over Susannah.

Robbie caused him more guilt than he could handle and had done so for more years than he

cared to count. His worry about his younger
brother stretched back as far as childhood when
their mother had left. Logan had done everything
he could to shield Robbie from the sudden loss of
their mother but he hadn't succeeded.

But when had he ever succeeded in a relationship of any kind?

Spending time with Layla opened up a new
world of connection and emotional intimacy—
that thing he had so assiduously avoided even in
his relationship with his fiancée. Getting to know
Layla on a deeper level had made him realise what
his relationship with Susannah had been missing.

It was hard to get his head around the fact they
were now officially married. It didn't seem real but
it was—he had the marriage certificate to prove
it. It was there in black and white.

On paper.

Layla looked up from examining the menu and
frowned. 'Is something wrong?'

Logan rearranged his features into an impas-
sive mask. 'No. Why?'

She closed the menu. 'You keep staring at me
and frowning.'

He gave an on-off smile. 'Sorry. I was thinking.'

'About what?'

'About us.' Even saying the word 'us' made
something in him sit up like a meerkat and take
notice.

She lowered her gaze to focus on the candle flickering on the table between them. 'It's kind of weird, isn't it? I mean, us being married.' Her gaze came back to his. 'But at least we've saved Bellbrae. That's what matters most.'

'It's not the only thing that matters,' Logan said. 'It's important you aren't too badly inconvenienced by our arrangement. I know a year is a long time but once we annul our marriage, you'll be free to move on with your life.'

The waiter approached with their drinks to take their meal order at that point. Logan tried not to think about Layla's life after their marriage ended. It would be strange seeing her marry someone else one day, perhaps even have a family. And if she moved away, she might not even be a part of Bellbrae any more. He couldn't imagine the Highland estate without her. The place would seem empty and colourless. Bleak.

Once the waiter had left, Layla picked up her wineglass and gently twirled the contents. 'My life is my business. That's all I care about. I want to be successful and self-sufficient.'

'Do you want a family as well one day?' Why was he asking when he didn't want to know? He didn't want to think about her as a mother of some other man's babies. It was none of his business what she did with her life after their 'marriage' came to an end. No business at all.

Layla lifted one slim shoulder in a tiny shrug, a frown forming between her downcast eyes. 'I'm not sure about that… Sometimes I think it would be wonderful to have a family. But other times I worry I could end up like my mother.' She flicked him a veiled glance. 'She married the wrong person. It not only ruined her life, it cut it short.'

Logan suspected there was a lot more to Layla's background than she had let on. Her guardedness around the subject of her childhood was testament to that. He knew she had been in a car accident that had claimed her parents' lives and caused her to be severely injured but he had a sense she hadn't had an easy life even before that terrible tragedy. 'Do you feel comfortable telling me what happened?'

Layla took a sip of wine and then placed her glass back on the table. Her features were a battleground of conflicting emotions as if she was deciding whether to reveal or conceal. But after a long moment, she started speaking in a voice that throbbed with conviction.

'My mother made a series of choices she might not have made if she'd been better supported. She came from a difficult background herself and then got caught up in a downward spiral of petty crime to lift herself out of poverty. One job would have broken the cycle, I'm sure of it. It would have given her independence and a sense of worth.'

'Is that why you're so keen to employ people from disadvantaged backgrounds?' Logan asked.

'Absolutely. They sometimes just need someone to believe in them.' She tapped her hand on the table for emphasis. 'To give them a fighting chance. My mother didn't have anyone in her life who believed in her potential.'

'What was your father like?'

A flash of anger lit her grey-green gaze and her mouth tightened. 'He was a brute and a bully but my mother got completely taken in by him because he promised to give her a better life. He said all the charming things she wanted to hear but they were empty promises. She thought because he called her "babe" that he actually loved her. But when he started to show his true colours, she didn't have the strength or self-esteem to stand up to him. The worst part was she drank and used drugs to escape his behaviour but in doing so became more like him.'

She released a ragged sigh and looked back at the candle flickering on the table, a hot flare of anger still smouldering in her gaze. 'If I can save one woman from what happened to my mother, then all the hard work and sacrifice will be worth it.'

Logan reached for her hand across the table and gave it a gentle squeeze. 'I think it's amazing what you're doing with your business. It's an honourable and compassionate approach that is innovative and enterprising. If you'd like me to help you with a business expansion plan, I can do that.'

She pulled her hand away and placed it on her lap, her expression defensive. Wary. 'I'm not completely incompetent. I've run my business for the last couple of years without going bankrupt.'

'I meant no offence, Layla. Good structure is vital in business expansion. A lot of small businesses fold when they try to expand too quickly. I have some skills in that area so the offer is on the table. Take it or leave it.'

Something softened in her tight expression. 'I'll think about it.'

A small silence passed.

'What was your mother like?' Layla asked.

The question blindsided Logan. He was so used to not thinking about his mother that it took him a moment to even bring her features to mind. Thinking about his mother made him think about himself and his brother as distraught children who didn't understand why Mummy wasn't coming back home. Why she never came back or never wanted to see them or even talk to them on the phone. It had been a brutal abandonment that had all but destroyed his father and changed Logan's and Robbie's lives for ever.

'She was beautiful and charming,' Logan said, stripping his voice of emotion. 'If my father hadn't destroyed all the photos of her, I could've shown you how beautiful she was.'

'Aunt Elsie told me how gorgeous she was,' Layla said. 'And that your father fell madly in love with her the moment he met her.'

'My father was completely captivated by her. They had a whirlwind courtship and I was born a few months after their wedding. I don't think it was ever a happy marriage but when Robbie came four years after me, things really started to come unstuck.' He picked up his wineglass. 'One day, I came home from school to find she had left.' He drank from his glass and put it back down on the table with an audible thud. 'That morning we'd had a mother. That afternoon we didn't. No goodbye. No note. Not even a phone call. She'd gone to live with her lover in America. I haven't seen her or heard from her since.'

Layla frowned in concern. 'It must have been devastating for you both. You were so terribly young—what? Both under ten?'

'Seven and four.' Logan's tone was flat. 'We didn't understand why she left. We both thought we must have done something to make her leave us.'

'I guess a lot of kids would think like that but surely you realise it wasn't anything to do with you or Robbie?'

He shifted the base of his wineglass a quarter-turn. 'It took me years to realise it wasn't us. It was her. She didn't have the capacity to bond. I heard she's been married three or four times since then.' He paused for a moment before adding, 'It was harder on Robbie. He was only four and missed her badly. He cried for weeks, months really. I did what I could to compensate but it wasn't enough—nowhere near enough. He needed his mother and no one else was going to fill the hole she left behind. Not even our father, who was struggling himself to cope.'

A frown pulled at her brow. 'You can't possibly blame yourself for Robbie's problems. You were left by your mother too and you didn't go off the rails.'

Logan gave her a grim look. 'I do blame myself. I was too lenient with him then and after our father died. Robbie was only fourteen and full of raging hormones and risk-taking behaviour, which was part puberty and part acting out his grief. My grandfather was too controlling with him and I tried to make up for it in other ways. It was a mistake to swing back too far the other way. I should've tried a more balanced approach.' He made a self-deprecating sound and added, 'I'm definitely not cut out for parenthood. Not with all the mistakes I've made with my brother.'

Layla leaned forward in her chair, her expression etched with concern. 'Logan, you're not to blame. I think you've been an amazing older brother. And you would make an amazing father. Robbie hasn't made great choices along the way but you've done nothing but support him and encourage him to make better ones. Even the way you've put your own life on hold to save Bellbrae is proof of that. It's not just your heritage that would've been lost but his as well. I know how your mind works—by marrying me you're ultimately protecting him from the shame of losing his family's ancestral home in a poker game.' She picked up her wineglass and sat back in her chair. 'And I admire you for it.'

Logan gave a twisted smile. 'Let's hope you still admire me after you've lived with me for a year.'

Something passed over her features—a shadow in her quickly averted gaze, the flicker of a tiny muscle near her cheek, a flattening of her mouth. 'That works both ways.' Her voice dropped half a semitone in pitch. 'Let's hope we remain friends.'

Logan raised his glass in a toast. 'To staying friends.'

CHAPTER SIX

LATER THAT NIGHT back at the villa after dinner, Layla joined Logan for a nightcap in the sitting room before going to bed. She found herself reluctant to allow the evening to end. She had learned so much about Logan over dinner—what motivated him, what drove him, what tortured him. She had revealed things about herself too, and hadn't felt as uncomfortable about doing so as she'd thought she would. There were still some things she didn't feel comfortable revealing—she couldn't imagine a time when she ever would. To anyone.

'Here we go,' Logan said, handing her a small glass with Cointreau on ice. 'One nightcap.'

'I really don't need any more alcohol,' Layla said. 'But since this is kind of a holiday...'

One side of his mouth tipped up in a half-smile. 'I bet you haven't had one of those in a while.'

'Like you can talk, Mr Workaholic.' Layla took a sip of her drink, giving him a wry look over the rim of her glass.

He sat on the sofa opposite hers and crossed one ankle over his other knee, one arm draped over the back of the sofa, the other holding his brandy and dry. 'Yes, well, I've never been much good at relaxing.' He took a sip of his drink, held it in his mouth for a brief moment before swallowing.

Layla kicked off her shoes and tucked her good leg underneath her, making sure her scars on her other leg were covered by her pantsuit trousers. 'When was your last holiday?'

A small frown carved into his forehead and he stared at the contents of his glass. 'I sometimes take an afternoon off when I'm away on a project.'

'An afternoon?' Layla snorted. 'Even I've managed better than that. I had a couple of weekends off in a row three months back.'

His lazy half-smile was back and it made something in her stomach slip. 'Go, you.' His voice was low and husky, his sapphire-blue eyes as dark as a midnight sky. 'Did you do anything special on those weekends off?'

Layla gave a laugh. 'Okay, you've got your *gotcha* moment. I did paperwork while I watched movies and ate pizza.'

His gaze was unwavering, his smile mesmerising. 'Looks like we both need lessons in how to relax.'

There was a sudden change in the atmosphere and Layla was the first to look away. Or maybe it was where her mind was taking her—to long, sleepy, relaxing lie-ins after making love. Her head resting on Logan's chest, his fingers playing with her hair, their legs entwined. That would be a good way to relax, surely? She sipped some more of her drink and hoped her cheeks weren't looking as hot as they felt.

'How about we stay on a few extras days here?' Logan said. 'We could explore some of the other islands. That is, if you can juggle your work commitments.'

Layla kept looking at the ice cubes in her glass rather than meet his gaze. An extended holiday in Hawaii would surely involve wearing a swimsuit, swimming, being surrounded by beautiful unscarred bodies on the beach. She could hardly relax under those circumstances. She would be waiting in dread for the whispered comments, the sideways glances, the *What happened to you?* questions. She leaned forward to put her glass on the coaster on the table in front of her. 'I don't know... Don't you have to check out your project in Tuscany?'

'It can wait a few more days.'

Layla could have used her work commitments as an excuse to get back to Scotland but the temptation to spend more time here with Logan was too hard to resist. She only had to send a couple of emails or make a few calls to make sure everything was ticking along efficiently with her cleaning business. She had some reliable staff who were more than capable of standing in for her. Why shouldn't she relax and enjoy herself for once? 'I guess it would be nice to see a bit more of Hawaii before we go home.'

'I'll make the arrangements.'

Layla tried but failed to disguise a yawn. 'Who knew eating and drinking could be so exhausting?' She carefully unfolded her leg from beneath her and rose from the sofa. 'I think I'll turn in. Thanks for a lovely dinner and…everything.'

He gave one of his rare smiles. 'You're welcome.'

Logan sat back and finished his drink once Layla had gone off to bed, wondering if he'd done the right thing in suggesting they extend their stay. He had originally planned to fly in and fly out once they were officially married. But he'd thought a few extra days might help both of them get used to their new circumstances before they went back to Bellbrae. Living together as man and wife, even on paper, was going to take some considerable adjustment, especially if they were to do it as authentically as they could by sharing the west tower suite. Besides, they were both hard workers who rarely took a break.

But her initial reluctance to stay on for a few

extra days made him wonder if it was not so much about spending time with him that troubled her but something else. The beach environment? Or maybe it was both. Not everyone enjoyed the beach, especially those with fair complexions like Layla, but he had seen her looking at other swimmers and sunbathers with a wistful look on her face.

His memory snagged on something…a memory from way back to when she had been a young teenager, not long after she had come to live with his family. He seen her watching him swim on the loch at Bellbrae. He'd pretended not to notice as he hadn't wanted to make her feel uncomfortable, but he'd been aware of her hiding in the shadows of the trees. When he'd brought his fiancée home, Layla had spied on them both. It had made Susannah annoyed but he'd forbidden her to say anything to Layla. And thankfully she hadn't. But he realised now he had never seen Layla swimming, not even in the indoor pool his grandfather had installed a few years ago after he'd had a hip replacement.

If Logan did nothing else on their 'honeymoon' he would help her overcome her reluctance to wear a swimsuit. Although just thinking about her in a swimsuit was enough to make his imagination run wild and his blood run hot. And the last thing his imagination needed was any encouragement. His willpower was having enough trouble as it was.

He had to remember—this wasn't a real honeymoon and it wasn't a real marriage.

Neither could it ever become one.

The following morning Layla woke to bright sunshine pouring through the windows of her bedroom. *Her* bedroom. Not *their* bedroom. Her first night as a married woman and she had spent it alone.

She heard sounds of Logan moving about in the suite outside her room and wondered if he too had found it odd to have spent their first night as a married couple in separate beds. Probably not. He was the one who had made the rules and was so determined to stick to them. And she had agreed to them, so why was she even mulling over their situation?

It was a sensible plan to keep their emotions out of the arrangement. It was wise for both of them to refrain from developing feelings that demanded more permanency. Her dream of finding someone to love her was just that—a dream. A fanciful dream that had little hope of being realised. And that secret little smouldering coal inside her? It needed a bucket of ice-cold reality thrown over it.

The fragrant smell of freshly brewed coffee tantalised Layla's nostrils and she threw off the bedcovers and slipped on a bathrobe to cover her satin pyjama set. She came out to the dining area of the luxury villa to find a colourful fruit platter and fresh croissants and rolls with butter and preserves laid out ready for breakfast.

Logan was pouring coffee into a cup and glanced up when she came in. 'Ah, Sleeping Beauty awakes. Coffee? Or would you prefer tea?'

'That coffee smells delicious,' Layla said, thinking he looked and smelled pretty damn delicious too.

His hair was still damp from a shower, his jaw was cleanly shaven and she could pick up a trace of the lemon and lime notes of his aftershave. He was dressed casually in white cotton shorts that set off the deep tan of his legs, his light blue T-shirt showcasing his well-toned chest. He looked rested, relaxed and ridiculously sexy, and her female hormones swooned.

He handed her a cup of steaming coffee. 'How did you sleep?'

Layla took the cup from him and breathed in the delicious aroma. 'Not bad...considering.' She took a sip of coffee, conscious of his unwavering gaze.

'Considering what?' He leaned one hip against the counter, holding his cup by the base.

Seemed she didn't need alcohol to get her tongue out of control. Some inner demon was goading her to point out the weirdness of their situation. A honeymoon with separate bedrooms. If that wasn't weird, what was? Layla put the cup down on the table and, pulling out a chair, sat and reached for a piece of golden pineapple. 'Considering it was the first night of my honeymoon.' She raised her fingers in air quotes over the word 'honeymoon', sending him an ironic look. 'It's not the way I imagined it as a child. Just saying...'

A ripple of tension crossed his features like sand blown by a breeze. 'You know my reasons for insisting our relationship stays on paper only.' His tone was schoolmaster stern, his gaze determined. 'I couldn't have made it any clearer.'

Layla took a bite of the juicy pineapple and chewed and swallowed. 'Yes, you've made it perfectly clear. And I'm totally fine with it.' *Was she?* Or was she just paying lip service? 'But I can't help wondering if it's not me you're trying to protect but yourself.'

He placed his cup on the table with a thud and frowned. 'Protect myself from what?'

She kept her gaze trained on his. 'From getting too close to someone. To feeling something for someone other than transient lust. You keep people at a distance. You've had plenty of casual lovers but you haven't had a live-in lover since you lost Susannah.'

He picked up the coffee pot and refilled his cup. 'You seem to know a lot about my love life.'

'But it's not a love life, is it? It's a lust life.'

He gave a rough laugh that held not a shred of humour. 'Works for me, sweetheart.' He raised his cup to his mouth and took a mouthful of coffee.

'It will work until one day it won't,' Layla said, picking up another piece of fruit—a wedge of pink watermelon this time—and placing it on her plate.

Logan pulled out the chair opposite hers and sat down and placed his coffee cup on the table, his forehead creased in a frown. 'Why is it so important to you how I live my life?'

Layla found it hard to hold his gaze. 'I've known you since I was a twelve-year-old kid. How could I not care about how you live your life?'

He gave a brief movement of his lips that fell short of a smile. 'I know you mean well, Layla, but, believe me, it's best if you don't care too much. Now, finish your breakfast. We have some serious sightseeing to do.'

Over the next couple of days Layla was left in no doubt about Logan's skill as a tour guide. He organised a tour of Haleakala National Park, located on Maui's inactive volcano, as well as visits to the Seven Sacred Pools of the Oheo Ravine and Makahika and Waimoko waterfalls. The lush rainforests with their towering, tumbling waterfalls were breathtaking, and Logan organised a private helicopter tour of the summit of the volcano, which gave stunning views over the crater and the whole island. He was sensitive without being patronising over the walks they took through the rainforest, and he always had a steadying hand at the ready if she gave any hint of losing her footing.

In the evenings they dined out at various restaurants, chatting over the day's sights, and then returned to the villa and retired to their separate quarters. It was clear Logan was doing everything he could to ensure their relationship remained platonic, but every now and again when he touched her as he helped her out of the car or took her hand over a rough part of a walk, her senses went into a frenzy.

The morning after their trip to the volcano Layla joined Logan at breakfast but instead of a day of touring, he suggested they stay at the villa for the day.

'It's going to be quite warm today and I thought you might appreciate a quieter day, relaxing around the pool,' he said, refilling her glass with fruit juice.

Layla had been pointedly ignoring the sparkling blue infinity saltwater lap pool on the seaboard terrace. Just like she ignored the beautiful indoor pool Angus McLaughlin had installed at Bellbrae to help him recover from a hip replacement a few years ago. 'I don't really enjoy swimming that much,' she said, picking up the glass of orange juice. 'But I'm happy to watch you do laps.' More than happy if she were to be perfectly honest. Hadn't she found secret pleasure in watching him for years?

Logan's gaze searched hers. 'Does it hurt your leg to swim?'

'No, it's just I...' She lowered her gaze back to the frothy juice in her glass. 'I'm a bit self-conscious about my scars.'

And I feel weirdly grateful I have them instead of my parents.

Of course she could never tell him. She couldn't tell anyone. It was too shameful to admit out loud.

'It will only be us here and you don't need to be shy around me.' His tone had a gentle note that ambushed her emotions. Could she do it? Could she reveal the marks on her body that signified the biggest turning point in her life?

Layla brought her gaze back up to his. 'It's been a long time since I've been in the water.'

Warmth shone in his eyes and his smile made her stomach do a somersault. 'I'll be there to help you.'

A short time later Layla came out to the pool area dressed in her green swimming costume with her sarong wrapped around her body and her hair tied back in a high ponytail. Logan was already in the pool, doing laps, and she stood in the shade of the shrubbery, watching him carve through the water with effortless grace and efficiency. He performed fluid tumble turns at each end, the water glistening on his tanned back and shoulders.

He stopped at the end closest to where she was standing and scraped his hair back away from his forehead. 'Hang on—I'll help you down the steps.' He placed his hands on the edge of the pool and launched himself out in one athletic movement that showcased his powerful biceps. He held out his hand, an encouraging smile tilting his mouth. 'You can do it, Layla. I won't let you slip.'

Wasn't she already slipping? Slipping into the dangerous waters of developing feelings she had promised she wouldn't feel. For anyone. How could she dare hope to be loved when even her own parents hadn't truly loved her? Their first love had been their addictions. But the more time she spent with Logan, the deeper her feelings grew. How could they not? It was like asking a flower not to bloom under healing, restorative sunshine.

Layla took a deep breath and let go of her sarong. It slipped to the pool deck at her feet, leaving her in nothing but the green costume. Her leg was criss-crossed with vivid white scars with dents where muscle had been grafted from her thigh to her calf. Her leg had been through a long hard battle to avoid being amputated and had only just won. And it showed.

She waited for the look of distaste, for the screwed-up expression of horror she had seen too many times to count. But Logan didn't show any of that. His eyes did an appraising scan of her body, lingering a little longer on the upthrust of her breasts and the cleavage its design highlighted, but there was no disgust in his gaze. There was desire. Desire that made her feel more of a woman than she had ever felt.

Layla took his outstretched hand and drew comfort and courage from the warm press of his fingers around hers. 'Okay…let's do this…' She walked with him down the slab steps of the pool into the silky embrace of the water. She was conscious of his strong male body right beside her, conscious of the fact he was wearing even less than she was. Conscious of the way her body responded to him in secret—the subtle increase in her heart rate, the little flickers of lust between her thighs.

Logan let go of her hand once she was standing waist deep in the water. 'Let the water support you. Don't fight it. Go with it.'

Layla bounced her feet off the bottom of the pool to put herself in a floating position, allowing the water to carry her weight. It was nothing short of bliss to be supported and she starting swimming a slow freestyle, because the gentle kicking motion was a little easier to manage with her leg. Tumble turns were beyond her capability, so she stopped at the end instead, caught her breath and then turned around and came back.

The sun was warm and the water shimmering as she passed through it. She was aware of every inch of her body the water touched, her muscles enjoying the pull and tug of exercise, her skin enjoying the caress of water.

She stopped at the end where Logan was waiting for her. She stood upright and smiled, flicking wet hair out of her face. 'I'm not quite up to your standard but thank you for encouraging me.'

'You look very at home in the water. Like a mermaid.' His tone had a husky edge and his dark blue eyes did another slow appraisal of her cleavage.

Layla knew she should turn around and keep swimming but something kept her frozen in place. Well, perhaps not quite frozen, for smouldering heat was travelling to every part of her body. Logan's gaze met hers and suddenly there wasn't a foot of space between them anymore. They were practically pelvis to pelvis with only a millimetre or two of water separating them. The magnetic pull of his body drew her inexorably closer until her breasts met the hard wall of his chest. His hands settled on each of her hips, his taut abdomen close enough for her to feel the jut of his growing erection.

Time stood still for an infinitesimal moment as

if an invisible hand had blocked the ticking hand of a clock. Tick. Tock. Stop.

Logan's head came down and his mouth met hers in a kiss that tasted of salt water, sun and male sensuality. Her mouth flowered open under the passionate pressure, her tongue meeting his in a sexy tangle that made shivers course down her spine. He moved against her and the hard nudge of his aroused body made her legs almost fold beneath her. He brought a hand to the small of her back, pressing her even closer to the throb of his flesh, his kiss deepening with a thrust of his tongue that was blatantly erotic.

Layla made a whimpering sound of encouragement, one of her hands sliding up to caress the back of his neck, the other his lean jaw. Escalating need pulsated through her entire body, her legs trembling with the sheer force of its unstoppable tide.

Logan's hand came to her swimsuit-clad breast, cupping it through the ruched fabric, but his touch still sent a shockwave of longing through her flesh. His arousal jutted against her feminine mound and he gave a deep rough-sounding groan against her mouth before finally lifting off.

He kept hold of her by the upper arms, his breathing heavy, his gaze hooded. 'I'm sorry.' His tone was full of self-reproach and he released her from his hold and stepped back with a brooding frown between his dark brows.

Layla licked her lips, relishing the taste of him still lingering there. 'You don't have to apologise. I—'

'I don't want to give you the wrong impression.' He dragged a hand over his face as if wanting to reset his features. 'It's not fair to confuse you by saying one thing and then doing another.'

'The impression I got was that you wanted to kiss me and enjoyed it as much as I did,' Layla said, challenging him to deny it with her unwavering gaze.

His gaze slipped to her mouth and he drew in a harsh-sounding breath, releasing it a whoosh of self-recrimination. 'I enjoyed it too damn much but it doesn't mean it's going to happen again.' He turned and launched himself out of the pool, spraying water droplets in an arc around him. 'I'm going to go for a run. I'll see you later.'

Layla sighed and sank under the water and began swimming again. Maybe a few punishing laps of the pool would tame her own frustrated desire.

Logan ran along the shoreline oblivious to the protestation of overused muscles. He was determined to beat this obsession with kissing Layla. He was the one who had made the rules—why was he finding it so damn hard to stick to them? Her mouth was a drug he had suddenly developed a hunger for and it was taking every bit of willpower he possessed to resist. What was it about her that made him so tempted to step over every boundary he had laid down?

But then a thought strayed into his mind... maybe he shouldn't resist. Maybe he could tweak the rules and see what happened. The thought sat down like an uninvited guest, put its feet up and got comfortable but Logan frogmarched it out of his head. He knew what would happen and he had to avoid it at all costs. He increased his pace along the sand, ignoring the burning sensations in his legs. Ignoring the heaving of his chest as he dragged in each gulping breath.

He hadn't forgiven himself for his last relationship disaster.

He couldn't—*wouldn't*—go there again.

CHAPTER SEVEN

LAYLA WAS TIRED after her swimming session and after a shower lay down on the bed to rest with one ear out to listen for when Logan returned from his run. But he must have been doing a marathon because every time she glanced at the clock by the bed, it had gone around another half an hour until finally she closed her eyes and drifted off to sleep...

Layla hadn't had the dream in years. She was in the back of the car, her parents were arguing in the front, with her father in the driving seat. The trees on the roadside were blurred by the speed her father was going. The car swerved and spun but her father corrected it, laughing manically and asking if they were wetting their pants yet. Her mother had stopped shouting back and was now shrunk into her seat, begging him to slow down in a whimpering voice, one side of her face already blackened by her husband's fist from the day before.

Layla saw the tree coming towards them, looming, looming. She screamed but it was too late. Too late. Too late…

Someone was trying to revive her. She could feel their hands on her shoulders and hear them calling her name. 'Layla. Wake up. You're having a bad dream. Wake up.'

But it wasn't the off-duty nurse or the paramedics who had been first on the scene that day. Layla opened her eyes to see Logan perched on the edge of her bed, his hands stroking back the hair that had fallen across her face.

'It's all right, I'm here. It was just a nightmare.' His voice was gentle and his touch soothing, anchoring her in the present, not the past.

Layla blinked away the terrifying images lingering in her head. She pushed herself upright into a sitting position, wincing against the light of the bedside lamp he had switched on. How long had she been sleeping? Hours and hours for it was now dark outside.

'Sorry. Gosh, I didn't realise it was night already. Did I wake you up?'

He took one of her hands and held it in his, stroking the back of it with slow, rhythmic movements. 'In bed but not asleep. I was going through some emails on my phone when I heard you call out.'

Layla peered at the bedside clock to find it was

close to midnight. 'Oh, I must have wrecked your dinner booking. Sorry. I didn't realise how tired I would be after swimming.'

'Can I get you something to eat or a drink of milk or something?'

She screwed up her face. 'Eww. I hate milk.'

His crooked smile transformed his features and made her heart do a little flip turn. 'I should have remembered that. What about fruit juice or herbal tea?'

'You don't have to fuss over me like I'm a little kid.' She plucked at the hem of the sheet with her fingers. 'I'm not hungry and I'm perfectly able to get myself back to sleep.' She kept her gaze lowered, conscious of his hair-roughened thigh so close to hers on the bed. Conscious of his stroking fingers on her hand, conscious of her body secretly reacting to his touch. Warmth spreading through her lower body, flickers of heat smouldering in her core.

He was dressed in boxer shorts but naked from the waist up. His lean and athletic build could have been no better advertisement for regular exercise. His pectoral muscles were toned and carved on his broad chest and the neat washboard ridges of the muscles on his abdomen spoke of man who was not afraid of pushing himself to the limit. It was all she could do to keep her hands to herself. Her fingers tingled with the desire to explore those toned ridges, to trace every hard contour.

'Do you want to talk about it? Your dream?' Logan's baritone voice was deep, calm and even and as soothing as his stroking fingers on the back of her hand.

Layla fixed her gaze on her hand encased in the shelter of his. Her skin was so pale against his tan, a reminder of all the essential differences between them. She hadn't been in a gym since rehab. She felt sick to her stomach at the thought. Too many reminders of the pain of trying to walk again, trying to be normal when normal was something other people took for granted and never had to question.

'I haven't had a nightmare in ages…' She chanced a glance at him to find him watching her with concern etched on his features. She lowered her eyes again and asked, 'Did I say anything while I was asleep?'

'You were calling out "Stop" repeatedly. I was worried we might've had an intruder. I came rushing in to find you thrashing on the bed in the throes of a nightmare.' His eyes were haunted with the stress of finding her so distressed. 'You were dreaming about the accident?'

Layla gave a small nod, her gaze still focussed on their joined hands. For years she had heard everyone refer to it as an accident. A chance thing, a driver error that had gone horribly wrong. Her memory might have been patchy for months after the crash but one thing she had always known was that it hadn't been a simple driver error. 'It wasn't an accident.' She brought her gaze back to his, her voice tight, her throat tighter. 'It was a deliberate car crash.'

Logan's hand stilled on hers, his eyes widening in alarm. 'What do you mean?' His tone was hollowed out, echoing with shock.

'My father wanted to kill us all. He drove the car into the tree because my mother told him she wanted to leave him.'

'Oh, Layla…' Logan's hand gripped hers as if he was trying to anchor her to him. To stop her being swept away by a tide of distressing memories. 'I can't imagine the panic and fear and pain you must have gone through. What a cowardly act. A disgustingly cowardly act.' His voice was full of cutting contempt for her father and deep concern for her.

Layla rolled her eyes in a tell-me-about-it manner. 'I certainly didn't win the father lottery, that's for sure. Or the mother one, although I think she would've had a much better chance of being a better mother if she hadn't married my father. His influence was destructive and damaging but by the time she got the courage to leave him, it was too late.'

Logan brushed back some imaginary hair off her forehead, his gaze steady and compassionate. 'The more I hear about your childhood, the more I admire you. You've done an amazing job of overcoming those terrible experiences.'

'I wouldn't have been able to do it without Aunt Elsie and your family's help,' Layla said. 'I know your grandparents were old-school Scots but their hearts were in the right place. I'm not sure how my life would've turned out if I'd stayed too much longer in foster care. I was there for a few weeks after I came out of rehab until Aunt Elsie got official guardianship of me. Some of those group homes were pretty terrifying. Damaged kids damaging other kids.'

She shook her head, trying to shake away the memories of the past.

'I know not all foster homes are awful but it's not the same as belonging to your own family.' She twisted her mouth and added, 'Not that my family was anything to crow about. My father was an angel in public but a bullying devil behind closed doors. He claimed to love us but he didn't know the meaning of the word.' She flopped back down against the pillows with a heavy sigh. 'Now I'm going to shut up about my childhood. I'm probably boring you.'

Logan turned her hand over and traced a slow line across her palm. 'You're not boring me at all.'

He locked his gaze on hers. 'In fact, I find you one of the most interesting and intriguing people I've ever met.' He drew a circle on her palm this time, the lazy movement of his finger sending shivers shooting up and down her spine.

Layla sucked in an uneven breath, her insides coiling with desire. She could see the same desire reflected in his sapphire-blue gaze. Desire that sent a current through the air like high-voltage electricity. She disguised a swallow, her heart picking up its pace, her pulse sprinting.

'Will you stay with me until I go back to sleep?' The question popped out almost before she knew she was going to say it. Her cheeks grew warm and she lowered her gaze and bit down on her lower lip, pulling her hand out of his and burying it under the sheet covering her lower body. 'Forget I said that. I'm old enough to get myself back to sleep.'

A silence ticked past. Tick. Tick. Tick.

Logan stood from where he was perched on the side of the bed, but he didn't leave. 'Scoot over,' he said, gesturing with his hand. 'I'll lie on top of the covers, though.'

Layla gave him a wry look. 'Don't you trust me?'

His expression was grim. 'I don't trust myself.'

It was a while before Layla fell back to sleep, but when she did it was deep and peaceful and dreamless. She woke as dawn was breaking, the sun stealing into the room, casting the bed in a golden beam of light as direct as a spotlight. She was lying on her side with the warm band of Logan's arm wrapped around her middle and one of his strong muscular legs flung over hers.

Sometime during the night, he must have joined her under the bedcovers but she had no clear memory of it. But now she was acutely aware of every part of his body where it was in contact with hers—his hard chest against her back, his strong thighs against her bottom, his arm across her waist. His head was resting on the top of hers, his breathing deep and even, each of his expelled breaths gently feathering her cheek.

He shifted position slightly, his arm tightening around her middle to draw her closer, his other hand skating over one of her breasts. Even through the light barrier of her silk pyjama top she could feel the outline of his broad male hand. Could feel the erratic leap of her pulse at his intimate touch. Could feel one of his hair-roughened thighs coming between hers, triggering a firestorm in her female flesh.

He gave a low sleepy murmur. 'Mmm…you feel nice.'

Layla knew she should wake him but she couldn't quite bring herself to do it. No one had ever held her like this. She had never experienced the warmth and comfort of a lover's touch. Was it wrong of her to want to break the rules he had laid down? She moved her legs experimentally against his, enjoying the feel of hard muscle and rough masculine hair against her smoother skin. His hand came back to her breast, cradling it with exquisite gentleness, his thumb rolling back and forth across her tightening nipple. Tingling sensations rioted through her body from her breast to her feminine core. Her breathing stalled, her belly swooped, her senses reeled.

Layla turned in his arms and he opened his eyes and swore not quite under his breath and released her and sat upright.

'Sorry.' His apology was brief, brusque and bruising to her ego.

'It's okay, Logan,' Layla said. 'You didn't do anything.'

He rubbed a hand down his face, the sound of his palm scratching across his morning stubble loud in the echoing silence. 'You should have woken me.' His tone was gruff, his eyes haunted with guilt and self-loathing.

Layla rolled her eyes. 'Oh, for goodness' sake. Why are you making such a big deal out of this? I enjoyed sleeping next to you. I enjoyed you holding me.'

His mouth was set in a taut line. 'This has to stop.' He sprang off the bed as if it had just poked him. '*I* have to stop.' He said it not quite under his breath, as if he was reminding himself, not her.

Layla pulled her knees up to her chest and wrapped her arms around them. 'Why do you have to stop?'

Whoa! What did you just say?

But her conscience wasn't listening and neither was her traitorous body. It was awake and wanting. Why shouldn't they explore the chemistry they shared? She could be casual about the time limit on their relationship, couldn't she? And maybe, just maybe the time limit would become irrelevant...

'You know why.'

'Because you feel you'd be betraying Susannah's memory?'

He frowned as if she had started speaking in a foreign language. 'No. Of course not. It's not about Susannah.'

'So it's me then. It's because it's me.' Layla couldn't quite remove the note of despondency in her tone.

He speared a hand through his hair and gave a rough sigh. 'It's me. Me not wanting to hurt you in the long run. Sex can be casual and God knows I've had plenty of it. But it wouldn't be casual between us. You know it wouldn't. It couldn't be. We already have an existing relationship and building sex onto that would make things way more complicated when the year is up on our marriage.'

Layla straightened her legs, crossed her ankles and folded her arms across her chest. 'But what if we decided not to end it after a year? We might decide to extend it for a bit long—'

'No.' His sharply delivered word was as stinging as a slap. 'We're not doing that, Layla. The rules are there for a reason.'

'I think the rules are there because deep down you want more than you'd like everyone to believe,' Layla said. 'You're still punishing yourself because of Susannah's death. It's understandable—it was a terrible tragedy to lose the love of your life. But you're entitled to have a life, even though hers has gone. You deserve to have some measure of happiness, even if it won't be on the same level as before.'

Logan muttered a thick curse and speared her gaze with his hard and glittering one.

'She wasn't the love of my life. There, that's shocked you, hasn't it? I thought I loved her at the start but then I started to feel less certain. I knew something wasn't right between us but I put it down to my preoccupation with work. I had a few big projects going on and I travelled a lot, and, to tell you the truth, I enjoyed coming home to someone who always seemed happy to see me. I think because I was away so much it took me longer to realise how unsuited we actually were. But when I finally realised, I *should* have ended it then and there, but her emotional fragility had started to worry me. I stupidly let our relationship limp along for the rest of the year but, as it turned out, I was right to be worried.'

Layla couldn't hope to conceal her shock at his embittered words. Her mouth was open, her eyes wide, her heart heavy for what he'd been through and the guilt that still plagued him. He had told her a few days ago that things hadn't been as perfect between him and Susanna as she had believed but she had still assumed he had loved his fiancée. Dearly loved her. Layla had always seen them as the ideal couple. They'd looked so good together, they had seemed to treat each other with the utmost respect, they came from the same world of wealth and privilege.

But had she *wanted* to see them that way? To fulfil her own girlhood romantic fantasy. Ignoring the subtle clues that things weren't quite as rosy and romantic as she'd wanted to believe.

But who knew how any relationship worked from the inside? Hadn't her childhood more than proved that? Happy Families was a game her father had played and played extremely well. Only those on the inside, behind the door closed to the public, knew what the true dynamics were.

Layla unfolded her arms and pushed the bedcovers off and got off the bed. It didn't matter that she was only dressed in cream silk pyjamas that draped her body contours rather too closely. He had seen her in far less in the pool the previous day. All that mattered was going to him, to offer some support and understanding, some compassion. She stood in front of him, never more conscious of their difference in height—she had to tilt her head right back to gain eye contact.

She touched him lightly on the arm, his masculine hairs tickling her palm, reminding her of yet another difference between them. 'I don't know what to say other than I'm so sorry things were so…so difficult…'

The tense lines around his mouth slackened on a heavily released breath and he took her hand from his arm and held it in his. His thumb moved across the back of her hand in an almost absent fashion, his eyes meshing with hers. 'The thing that haunts me is—' he winced, as if recalling the memory pained him '—I think she knew I was going to call off our engagement eventually. I was waiting for the right time, when I thought she could handle it better emotionally. But I didn't know about her eating disorder—apparently, she had it before we met. I still can't forgive myself for not realising how ill she was. I probably made her illness worse by not being fully present in the relationship for all those months.'

Layla moved closer without even realising she was doing it. It seemed natural to be standing so close to him, natural to put her arms around him and even more natural to hug him. His arms came around her—warm, strong, male arms that made everything feminine in her body shiver in delight.

'We're all good at hiding things we're ashamed of, and unfortunately eating disorders are high on the list,' she said, resting her head against his chest. 'I know it's useless me telling you not to blame yourself, but you did what you could based on the information you had at the time. You stayed with her and supported her as best you could for far longer than most men would've done.'

Logan began a gentle stroking of the back of her head, each downward movement of his hand making the base of her spine melt. Her breasts were pressed against the broad wall of his chest, her pelvis so close to his, a sensation spread through her lower body like a slow flow of warm treacle. The stirring of his male flesh against her sent a dart of lust between her legs, her inner core pulsating, contracting with a tender ache.

He eased back to look down at her, his eyes so dark it was hard to tell his pupils from the deep blue of his irises. The haunting shadows in his gaze had faded and now his eyes contained a new energy—an intense energy that spoke of attraction, desire, need.

Logan framed her face with his hands, his touch so gentle it made a closed space inside her chest suddenly flare open. 'I told myself this wasn't going to happen.' His voice was as rough as gravel, deep as a base chord with a side note of longing. His gaze dipped to her mouth, lingering, smouldering. 'You deserve better than what I can offer. Much better.'

'But what if I'm happy with what you're offering?' Layla laid one of her hands on the hard plane of his chest, the other on his richly stubbled jaw. 'What if I want you to kiss me and make love to me, even if it's only for the duration of our marriage?' She could scarcely believe she was offering herself on such stripped-down terms. What had happened to her dream of lifelong love? What had happened to her secret belief in the happy-ever-after fairy-tale?

Logan had happened, that was what. Her need for him overrode every other thought.

He closed his eyes in a tight blink as if calling on whatever internal willpower he possessed but finding it missing. 'I don't want to hurt you. I seem to have a particular talent for hurting people I care about. I don't want you to be one of them.'

Layla linked her arms around his neck, her fingers playing with the dark brown ends of hair that brushed against his neck. 'The way you'll hurt me is to not kiss me, to not want me the way I want you. But you do want me, don't you? Or am I just imagining it?'

He placed a hand at the base of her spine and drew her against the evidence of his arousal, his eyes glinting. 'You're not imagining it. I want you so badly it's making me crazy. Ever since I saw you packing up my grandfather's things in the north tower, it was like a switch turned on inside me. I can't seem to turn it off.'

Layla stepped up on tiptoe, bringing her mouth closer to the slow descent of his. 'I don't want you to turn it off. Not now. Not yet.' *Not ever.*

His head came down, a deep groan coming from the back of his throat as their lips met in an explosive kiss. Heat flared, flames of lust licking along Layla's flesh like wildfire in a tinder-dry forest. His tongue met hers, playing, duelling, teasing, dancing. His fingers splayed through her hair, his head tilting so he could deepen the kiss, his lower body pressed to hers in passionate desperation. She instinctively moved against his hot hard heat, her body delighting in the potency and power of his body. It was erotic, it was exciting, it was exhilarating to feel the throb and pound of his blood in such an intimate manner. She had never been so close to a man before. Her teenage date that ended so humiliatingly hadn't been anything like this.

This was adult attraction in full flare—mutual attraction that sent fizzing sensations to every secret corner of her body. Her spine loosened like molten candlewax, her legs trembled, the backs of her knees tingled, her pulse raced.

Logan placed his hands on her hips and raised

his mouth off hers, his breathing ragged. 'It's not too late to stop this. You have to be sure—*I* have to be sure you really want this.'

Layla stroked the side of his face with her palm. 'I want you, Logan.' Her voice was whisper-soft but no less determined. 'You turned a switch on in me too. I want you to make love to me.'

His hands tightened on her hips and for a sinking moment she thought he was going to put her from him, but then he brought her closer again—close enough for her to feel the imprint of his erection against her belly. His head came back down and his mouth met hers in a drugging kiss that made the hairs on the back of her neck pirouette.

He tore his mouth away after a long moment. 'Wait. Condom.' He left her briefly to go to the other bedroom where his things were stored.

Layla held her breath the whole time he was away, fearful he would change his mind about making love to her. But he came back carrying the tiny foil packet, his eyes smouldering as soon as they met hers. 'Still okay about this?'

'More than okay.'

Somehow, they made it back to the bed in a series of stop-starts where the kiss deepened, intensified, electrified. Where their breathing became laboured, their need escalating. Where his hands skated over her aching flesh in a voyage of discovery, and hers did the same, with boldness she hadn't known she possessed.

A distant part of Layla's mind told her she should tell him she was a virgin but she couldn't bring herself to do it. She didn't want to risk him changing his mind—she suspected he would call an immediate halt to their lovemaking. He would see her lack of experience as yet another reason to keep their marriage on paper. But she wanted him to be her first lover. Why shouldn't it be him? Someone who had known her for many years, who had seen her grow from girl to woman.

Someone she trusted, cared about, respected. *Loved.*

Of course she loved him. She wasn't sure when it had started. It had been a gradual awakening, a slow burn of interest and attraction that had morphed into a persistent and powerful emotion.

Logan laid her down on the bed and came down beside her. He slowly undid the buttons on the front of her pyjama jacket, the feel of his fingers against her bare skin making her shiver in anticipation. He peeled the silky jacket from her shoulders and his breath audibly hitched. 'You're so perfect, so beautiful…' he said, his hand cupping her right breast, his touch sending tingles shooting through her body.

Perfect? That was a word Layla wasn't used to associating with herself. Neither was the word beautiful, but right then she felt like a beautiful woman. A beautiful desirable woman who was embracing her sexual power for the first time.

She explored the toned muscles of his chest, her fingers finding his hard, flat male nipples. His chest was lightly dusted with dark hair that narrowed down to a tantalising trail that disappeared below the waistband of his boxer shorts.

Logan brought his mouth to her breast, closing his lips over her budded nipple, his tongue flicking the sensitised nub. It was a pleasurable torture, the sensation of his warm mouth and raspy tongue sending her into raptures of delight.

Until now her breasts had been nothing but breasts. On the small side, occasionally a little tender around period time, but just breasts. No more, no less.

Now they were an erogenous zone—an intense pleasure spot that made her proud to be a woman.

Layla shuddered when he took her other breast in his mouth, the same riotous sensations shooting through her body from chest to core and back again. A hollow ache began spreading in her lower limbs, a heavy dragging sense of need.

'I want you…' Her voice was a breathless plea, her hands instinctively reaching between them for the jut of his erection.

'Same goes.' He groaned and brought his mouth

back to hers in a kiss that spoke of burning, building, blatant passion.

One of his hands began to slide her pyjama trousers down but Layla suddenly froze, placing her hand over his. 'Wait.' The room was brightly lit now with morning sunshine. The water in the pool yesterday had provided a bit of a cover, not much but a bit. But now there was nowhere to hide. Even with the blinds and curtains drawn, her scars would be clearly visible.

He frowned at her in concern. 'Did I go too fast? Do you want to stop?'

She swallowed and pressed her lips together, not quite able to hold his gaze. 'I don't want to stop but I'm worried you will want to when you see my scars up close.'

'Oh, sweetheart…' His breath came out on a jagged sigh. 'Do you really think I would be so insensitive?'

She gave a half-shrug. 'My scars have turned off men before.' Only one, but it had been enough to stop her dating since.

His frown deepened. 'Then you've been dating the wrong men. You're a beautiful young woman who's survived a terrible car crash. No one should judge or shame you for bearing the scars of a tragedy you were caught up in. If they do, then it says more about them than it does you.'

Layla knew what he said was intellectually

sound but she had lived experience of being judged and shamed by people who couldn't stomach her scars. There were times when she couldn't stomach them herself. She had spent years of her life avoiding intimacy, making excuses not to get into the dating scene—she was always too busy with work, too tired to indulge in late nights at clubs or parties.

But the real reason was what her scars represented. Not just the culmination of years of abuse and neglect now worn on her body like an indelible brand. Those scars represented her guilty secret—the secret relief that she had lost her parents and not her leg.

How could she ever tell anyone?

'It's just hard…you know?' Layla blinked away the sting of tears. 'Everywhere I look I see perfect bodies, especially in a place like Hawaii. Before yesterday, I hadn't been in a swimsuit since I was at the rehab clinic. I used to love swimming, but even at the clinic therapy pool, other patients stared at me like I was some sort of freak show.'

Logan brushed some strands of hair off her face, his gaze grave and yet tender. 'Your scars are a part of you, but they aren't *you*. You are so much more than that. So much more.'

Layla touched his mouth with her fingers. 'Kiss me. Make love to me. Please?'

His mouth tilted in a slow sexy smile. 'With pleasure.'

CHAPTER EIGHT

LOGAN'S MOUTH CAME back to hers in a kiss that melted away Layla's lingering doubts and fears. It was almost worth the long years of celibacy to have Logan be the first one to introduce her to the delights of the flesh. He moved from her mouth back to her breasts, caressing each one until her back was arching off the bed. He drew her pyjama trousers down, leaving a trail of kisses on each part of her exposed flesh. When he came to the jagged scars that were carved like runnels in her flesh, he was especially tender and it made tears spout in her eyes and her throat tighten with emotion.

He traced the feminine seam of her body with a lazy finger, his eyes glittering darkly with lust. 'Tell me if I do anything you don't like or don't feel comfortable doing.'

'I love what you're doing.' Layla could barely speak for the sensations rippling through her.

He kissed his way down her body from her

breasts to the swell of her mound. She sucked in a breath, her legs turning to water as his lips gently parted her tender folds. Layla was in two minds— one to stop him out of her shyness at such an intimate caress and the other to just lie back and enjoy every pulse-racing moment. She chose the latter. His lips and tongue sending her on a sensual roller-coaster that catapulted her into a vortex of dizzying sensations. Sensations that coursed through her body in waves and pulses and delicious flickers, finally leaving her in a state of utter bliss and relaxation.

Never had she felt so in tune with herself, so free of the burdensome worry of how her broken body looked. Her body felt amazing, beautiful and sexy and capable of giving and receiving pleasure.

How could she not be thrilled it was Logan who had transformed her, awakened her to her sensual potential?

'Oh, wow…' Layla said on a breathless sigh.

Logan planted a soft kiss on her lips and then lifted off to mesh his gaze with hers. 'It will only get better once we get used to each other.' He kissed his way from her neck to her breasts, stroking her with his tongue, grazing her with the gentle tug of his teeth, sending her senses into another rapturous tailspin.

Layla explored him with her hands, shyly at first but becoming more comfortable with the hard contours of his body that were so exotically, erotically different from her own. His arousal was thickened with the same need she could feel throbbing in her own body.

His breathing became more hectic under her touch, his eyes dark and lustrous with desire. He positioned himself between her legs, taking his own weight on his elbows, his body poised to possess her. 'It's not too late for second thoughts. We can stop if you don't want to go any—'

Layla pushed her finger against his lips to stop him speaking. To stop him talking himself out of making love to her. 'I don't want to stop. I want you to make love to me. You *want* to, don't you?'

His mouth came up in a rueful half-smile. 'You surely don't doubt it? Can't you feel what you do to me?'

She could and she loved feeling it. Loved feeling desirable and feminine and sensually powerful for the first time in her life. 'Don't leave me hanging like this,' she whispered against his mouth. 'I need you.'

Logan made a sound deep in his throat and captured her mouth with his in a kiss that spoke of the feral rumble of passion throbbing in his blood. The same passionate throb she could feel in her lower body, the ache and drag of tender muscles crying out for intimate friction. His body nudged her entrance, gently parting her, and she opened herself to him, her shyness falling away, replaced by her escalating need to feel him inside her. His first thrust was shallow, restrained, careful, as if he was reluctant to allow his desire too much freedom.

Layla arched her spine, welcoming him deeper into her body by placing her hands on his toned buttocks. He thrust into her with a guttural groan, his pelvis moving in primal motion with hers. She felt a tiny sting of pain, a slight tug of resistance when he went deeper and she suppressed a gasp, hoping he hadn't noticed.

He suddenly stilled his movements. 'Did I hurt you?' His voice contained a deep chord of concern, his gaze searching hers.

'Of course not.' Layla smiled and stroked the side of his face with her hand. 'I'm just getting used to the feel of you.' She held her breath, hoping he wouldn't see through her little white lie. She didn't want him to stop making love to her, not while her body was aching and throbbing for more stimulation.

His eyes moved between each of hers, dipping every now and again to her mouth, his breathing still uneven, his body still encased in hers. 'I'll take it a little more slowly. But tell me if you're not comfortable at any time.'

'I'm perfectly comfortable.' Layla moved beneath him, rocking her body to encourage him to keep moving. Her body was used to him now, her intimate muscles wrapping around him, welcoming him, delighting in his strength and potency.

He slowly began to thrust, his movements measured and controlled. Layla's excitement grew as his body within hers triggered flickers of heat through her female flesh. The erotic motion of their bodies working together in perfect harmony was like a complicated but beautiful dance she hadn't realised she had known the steps to until now. The choreography of their movements was instinctive, intuitive, intensely arousing. Her senses soared, her desire leapt, her blood hummed and thrummed like the rhythmic backbeat of a musical score.

His mouth came back to hers in a long, drugging kiss that ramped up her passion for him like fuel flung on a naked flame. Their tongues met, tangled, mated, moved with the same perfect symmetry as their bodies. His hands caressed the swell of her breast, the curve of her waist, her thigh and then he found the slippery secret heart of her. The soft stroking of his fingers on her most intimate flesh made her gasp and writhe and shudder as the orgasm swept over her in pulsating waves. Waves that fanned out from her core to the far reaches of her body, making every cell of her body vibrate with aftershocks of pleasure.

Logan's release followed hers with a series of deep urgent thrusts, his face buried into the side of her neck, his breathing as erratic as hers. He groaned and the tension in his body left him, making him slump against her.

Layla held him to her, not wanting him to pull away, wanting, needing to feel the warm embrace of his body for as long as possible. Their breathing came back to normal almost in unison, their entwined limbs rearranging themselves as if they had been doing it since time began.

After a long moment, Logan raised himself on one elbow to look down at her, his fingers idly playing with some tendrils of her hair. His features were cast in relaxation and the afterglow of pleasure and she had never seen him look more heart-stoppingly attractive.

'I'm having my own *Oh, wow* moment here.' His eyes were dark and warm, his voice pitched low, a lazy smile tilting his mouth. 'Make that *oh, wow* to the power of ten.'

An internal glow radiated through Layla's body at his words. She drew a line from the bridge of his nose to the well-defined philtrum ridge below and then traced his mouth. 'It was pretty amazing, wasn't it? Or maybe it's always amazing for you?'

He coiled a tendril of her hair around his finger, releasing it so it bounced against her cheek. He tucked the curl behind her ear, his expression undergoing a subtle change like the slow drift of clouds across the sky.

'I'm not the sort of man to kiss and tell, but sometimes sex works well and other times…' he twisted his mouth '…it's best left as a one-off.' He eased away to dispose of the condom in the bathroom, and Layla rolled onto her side, her eyes drinking in the long lean line of his back and taut buttocks and strong thighs.

She sighed and stretched like a sleepy cat, her limbs feeling so relaxed it was as if her bones had been removed. But then she happened to notice a mark on the bedlinen where she had been lying and her heart came to a screeching halt. She scrambled into a sitting position, hauling the bedcovers up to cover the bloodstain and her nakedness just as Logan came back into the bedroom.

'Is something wrong?' he asked, frowning.

'Um…no, I—I just feel a bit embarrassed about being…naked.' Layla bit her lip and couldn't hold his gaze.

Logan came over to the bed and sat down beside her. He pushed the fall of her hair back behind her shoulders, his hand going to the small of her back in a warm circular caress. 'I saw the blood on the condom. You don't have to be embarrassed about having your period.'

Layla swallowed, her heart beating so loudly she could feel it in her ears. 'I'm not having my period.' The words fell into the room like a loaded grenade, fizzing in the sudden silence.

Logan's hand stilled on her back, his body stiffening as if snap-frozen, his expression etched in shock as realisation slowly dawned. 'You were a...a *virgin*?' His voice was so hoarse it came out like the screech of tyres on gravel. He shot off the bed and shoved a hand through his hair, looking at her in alarm. 'Why didn't you say so?'

Layla pulled the bedcovers closer. 'It's not like it's a disease.'

He let out a short sharp swearword. 'I *hurt* you. You should have told me so I could've—'

'Could've what?' Layla shot back. 'Stopped? Not made love at all? Go on, admit it—you would never have made love with me if I'd told you I was a virgin.'

He closed his eyes in a slow blink and swore again. He turned away and snatched up his trousers from where they were lying on the floor and stepped into them with such force she was sure they would rip. The sound of his zipper going up was as savage as another bitter curse.

'You made me believe you were experienced,' he said, reaching for his shirt and shoving his arms through the sleeves. 'You lied to me, if not outright then by omission.'

'Stop making such a big issue out of it. It was just sex.'

'It was damn well not just sex.' His tone was gruff, his gaze diamond-hard. 'You knew I was uneasy about making our marriage a real one because we don't fit the criteria for a one-night stand.' He tucked his shirt into his trousers with rough movements. 'I can't believe how screwed up this is. I hurt you enough to make you bleed.' He rubbed a hand down his face, dragging and distorting his features.

'You didn't hurt me,' Layla said. 'It was the tiniest sting—I hardly even noticed it and everything was fine after that. More than fine—wonderful.'

Logan came over to the bed and sat beside her but he clamped his hands to his thighs as if he was worried they might touch her of their own accord. 'Why were you still a virgin? Was it a deliberate choice or something else?' His tone lost its sharp edge, his expression softening from its harsh lines of self-recrimination.

Layla looked down at her hands clasped around her bent knees. 'I came close once to having sex when I was a teenager but the guy got cold feet when he saw my leg. He made me feel terrible about my body. I've avoided any sort of intimacy ever since.'

Logan scrunched up his face as if suffering from an internal pain. He let out a sigh and took one of her hands in his, the gentle press of his fingers against hers making her eyes well with tears. 'I'm sorry you've had such an awful experience.

That kid was a jerk for making you feel that way. You're beautiful and desirable and deserve to be treated with nothing but respect. But don't you see how what happened just now makes *me* feel like a jerk? I hurt you and that's the last thing I wanted to do to you or to anyone.'

Layla looked into his frowning gaze and sighed. 'I'm sorry. I was embarrassed, that's all. I mean, what girl these days gets to the age of twenty-six without having had sex? It made me feel like a pariah. Completely out of step.'

He gave her hand another squeeze. 'One day you'll find what you're looking for. Someone who can give you the security and longevity that enriches a physical relationship.' He rose from the bed and moved some distance away, his expression still wrought with lines of tension.

'What if I'm not looking for that right now?' Layla asked. 'What if I only want a fling to get some experience under my belt? What would be wrong with you being the person who helps me with that?'

He turned back to look at her, his fisted hands clenching and unclenching by his sides as if he was fighting the urge to come back and haul her into his arms. 'I'm trying to do the right thing by you, Layla. I try to do the right thing by everyone I care about and yet I always seem to screw up.'

'I'm sorry for not telling you…'

He approached her again, his expression wistful, the gentle stroke of his finger down the slope of her cheek making her heart swell to twice its size. 'None of this is your fault, sweetheart. None of it.'

Layla grasped his wrist and turned his hand over so she could plant a soft kiss to the middle of his palm. 'I'm glad it was you. I mean, that you were my first lover.'

His eyes smouldered for a long moment, his fingers entwining with hers. 'It was pretty damn good, wasn't it?' His voice had a side note of gravel that made her inner core tingle.

'Does that mean you're going to tweak the rules?'

A shadow drifted through his gaze and he let out a sigh and released her hand. 'Let's not get too far ahead of ourselves.' He softened it with a crooked smile. 'I couldn't have asked for a more generous and responsive lover. But there are consequences to factor in if we take this any further.'

'I know,' Layla said. 'But I'm prepared to accept the consequences if you are.'

He traced the line of her lower lip with his finger, his expression sobering once more. 'Thing is…it's kind of scary how little I care about the consequences right now, which is why I'm going to sleep in the spare room. We both need some space to think clearly.'

Layla flopped back down on the pillows once he left the room. She didn't need space. She needed him.

Logan gave up on any notion of sleeping for the rest of the night. He paced one of the spare bedrooms with his thoughts as tangled as fishing line. He could not forgive himself for not realising Layla's lack of experience. How could he have been so blind? In hindsight, all the clues were there. He had never heard any mention of a boyfriend, he had never seen her bring anyone home to Bellbrae, and although he knew little of her life in Edinburgh, she had given him the impression she was experienced with her misleading and ambiguous comments about her past love life. And he'd fallen for it, because he'd *wanted* an excuse to sleep with her. That was the part of his conscience he was struggling with the most. He had broken his own rules—the rules he had instated to protect her from unnecessary hurt.

And he had gone and done it anyway.

He sucked in a jagged breath and released it in a rush. He had done it because ever since that day in the north tower, he had felt something shift in their relationship. A tectonic shift. He couldn't be in the same room as her without feeling the subtle change in energy. Sensual energy that tingled and tightened his skin and made him want and want and want with an ache that wouldn't go away, no matter how hard he tried to ignore it.

And that was another tripwire in his conscience— he'd enjoyed every pulse-racing minute of their lovemaking. It had been off the scale in terms of pleasure. Satisfying in a way sex hadn't been for him for years. The intuitive connection of their bodies, the rhythm and timing of every movement had felt so natural, so fluid and free and phenomenal it still rang in his flesh like a struck tuning fork.

Logan walked to the windows overlooking the ocean, trying to distract himself with the view, but it was no good.

How could you have not known? What were you thinking? You hurt her.

He wanted to blank them out but a perverse part of him relished in the self-flagellation. It was no more than he deserved. He had once thought he was pretty good at reading people but not now. His disastrous and tragic relationship with his fiancée had taught him otherwise. And now this situation with Layla had only reinforced it.

He was rubbish at relationships. How could he hope to change that abysmal track record? Was there any point even trying?

The journey back to Scotland was painfully silent. Layla tried once or twice to engage Logan in conversation on the flight but he only answered in monosyllables and seemed preoccupied with his thoughts. He rarely touched her. In fact, he seemed to be avoiding all contact, even eye contact. Was he still regretting their lovemaking? He had been so tender and considerate afterwards that a hope had sprouted in her chest that maybe he would agree to deepening their relationship. Had he weighed up the potential consequences and decided it wasn't worth it?

That *she* wasn't worth it?

On the drive back to Bellbrae from Inverness airport, Logan drove with clenched hands and jaw, his forehead creased in a perpetual frown, which didn't nurture her fledgling hope one little bit.

'You know, we're not going to be very convincing as a married couple if we don't even exchange a few polite words now and again,' Layla said.

He flicked her a glance. 'Sorry. Did you say something?'

She gave a humourless laugh. 'I've been trying to make conversation with you ever since we left Honolulu. You've barely spoken four or five words to me. I guess the honeymoon is definitely over, then?'

He flinched at the word 'honeymoon' and his hands tightened like clamps on the steering wheel. 'I can't tell you how much I regret what happened. I hate myself for hurting you.'

'I wish you'd stop making such an enormous

deal about it. So what if we had sex? Even perfect strangers have sex with each other. Besides, no harm has been done.'

His gaze swung her way again. 'Hasn't it?'

'Of course not.' Layla surreptitiously squeezed her legs together, secretly enjoying the pull of still tender muscles that his intimate presence had caused. She had relived their lovemaking numerous times, remembering each touch, each caress, each kiss that had set her flesh on fire and left it thrumming with pleasure. Her body ached to feel his presence again, to experience more of his magical lovemaking. To explore the sensuality that had erupted so naturally between them and shown her a world of heady and erotic delights she hadn't known existed. She kept her hands planted on her lap but she longed to place her hand on his thigh like a lover would do.

The rest of the journey continued in mutual silence but just as they approached the long driveway leading to the Bellbrae estate, Logan let out a stiff curse, not quite under his breath.

'What's wrong?' Layla asked.

'That's Robbie's new car,' he said, indicating the flashy red sports car ahead of them on the driveway. 'God only knows how he's paying for it. It's worth five hundred thousand euros at least.'

Layla looked ahead to see the sports car's wheels spinning over the gravel, spraying stones out to each side and it reminded her yet again of the stark differences between the two brothers. Logan was steady, reliable and cautious, someone who thought before he acted. Robbie, on the other hand, leapt before he looked, reacted rather than reflected, took risks and suffered little or no remorse for his reckless actions.

'Have you spoken to him since we…got married?' Layla asked. The word was still a novelty to her, even though she wore his ring on her left hand.

'I sent an email. I gave up on the phone—he hardly ever gets back to me when I call or text.' The weariness in Logan's tone spoke of a long and frustrating history between him and his younger brother. 'I told him we'd formed a relationship and decided to get married.'

Nerves in Layla's stomach unfurled and fluttered their razor-sharp wings. It was going to be difficult to convince his brother their marriage was genuine when Logan was so determined to keep his distance from her. 'But he would have seen the will, surely? Won't he have already put two and two together?'

'It's immaterial what he thinks. It doesn't change the fact our marriage is legal.'

Layla bit down on her lower lip. 'I'll try not to let you down.'

He flashed her the briefest of rueful smiles but

it didn't take the shadows out of his eyes. 'That seems to be my job. Letting people down.'

Logan helped Layla out of the car a short time later, placing his arm around her waist as his brother sauntered over to them. She nestled against his side and he caught a whiff of the flowery fragrance of her hair, stirring his senses, making him long to bury his head in those silky chestnut tresses as he had when they had made love. He tried to block the images of that night but they flashed up in his mind, causing his blood to pound and thicken, dragging at his lower body with a tight primal ache.

Robbie swept his gaze over them with an elevation of his eyebrows. 'Well, well, well, what have we here? Congratulations, Layla. You've landed yourself quite a catch. For a simple charwoman, that is.'

Logan felt Layla stiffen beside him and he wanted to thump his brother for being such a snobbish jerk. He drew her closer to his side and sent his brother a warning look. 'If you don't treat my wife with respect you won't be welcome here, Robert. Got that?'

'Your wife?' Robbie threw his head back and laughed. 'You expect me to believe you two are the real deal?'

'We have the documentation to prove it,' Logan

said. 'Now, if you'll excuse us. Layla is tired from travelling and—'

'I bet you put the old man up to it,' Robbie said, addressing Layla with a curl of his lip. 'You've always had the hots for my big brother. But he would never have looked at you without some serious arm twisting. And it doesn't get more serious than his precious Bellbrae hanging in the balance.'

Logan was ashamed to hear his brother voice his own earlier thoughts over his grandfather's changes to his will. And as to Layla's interest in him, well, it was more than reciprocated. And if he were to be honest with himself, that spark of attraction had started way earlier than the afternoon in the north tower. Way, way earlier.

'Layla had nothing to do with Grandad's will being changed. If anyone is to blame for that it's me. I've taken way too long to get on with my life after losing Susannah. But the time is right now and I can't think of a better person to marry than Layla, who loves this place as much as I do.'

'Personally, I don't get what either of you see in this place,' Robbie said, throwing the castle a look of distaste. 'It's old and cold and too far away from any action. You're welcome to it. And to each other.'

Layla's cheeks were a bright shade of pink and yet he was proud of the way her chin came up and her grey-green gaze stared his brother down. 'I know our marriage must've come as a complete surprise to you, Robbie, but Logan and I have always been friends. I hope, in time, you can be happy for us.'

Robbie's smile was cynical. 'I've seen the will. I know what this is—a marriage of convenience to secure Bellbrae. My brother will never love you, Layla. He's not capable of it.'

'You're wrong,' Layla said. 'He's capable of much more than you give him credit for.'

'I think it might be time for you to leave,' Logan said to his brother. 'We're still on our honeymoon and three's a crowd and all that.'

Robbie tossed his car keys in the air and deftly caught them, his expression mocking. 'I give you guys a year, tops.'

That's all I want, Logan thought.

And Logan led Layla into the castle without a backward glance as his brother roared down the driveway with a squeal of tyres over the gravel.

CHAPTER NINE

LAYLA LOOKED AT Logan once the door was closed on their entry into the castle. His expression was thunderous and a muscle kept flicking in his cheek.

'Are you okay?' she asked.

He let out a rough-edged sigh and shrugged himself out of his jacket and hung it on the coat rack near the entrance. 'I'm sorry about that. My brother can be a prize jerk sometimes. Most of the time, actually.'

'It's okay.' She began to unbutton her own coat. 'Our relationship must've come as a bit of a shock. I mean, you and me? It's a bit of a stretch to think you would ever be—'

His hand came down in a gentle press on the top of her shoulder, his expression softening. 'Don't keep doing that. You're a beautiful and desirable woman and if things were different, I would…' He pressed his lips together as if determined not to voice the words out loud.

'Would what?' Layla's voice was barely more than a whisper.

His navy-blue eyes darkened and his other hand came down on her other shoulder. She wasn't sure who moved first but suddenly they were standing almost chest to chest and hip to hip. The quality of the air changed—a tension was building, crackling, fizzing like a current of electricity singing along a wire. His gaze dipped to her mouth and she heard the intake of his breath. Held her own breath as his head lowered as if in slow motion, down...down...down...

'Oh, sorry to be a gooseberry!' Aunt Elsie's cheery lilt sounded from the right of the foyer. 'How did the wedding and honeymoon go?'

Logan stepped back but kept one of Layla's hands in his. 'It was short but wonderful.'

Aunt Elsie beamed like she was intent on solving an energy crisis for the whole of Scotland. 'Well, it wasn't long enough to my way of thinking, which is why I'm going to go on a wee holiday of my own to give you two lovebirds some space.'

Lovebirds? If only. And since when had her great-aunt ever left Bellbrae?

Layla looked at her great-aunt as if she had just said she was going to tap dance on the castle roof. Naked. 'But where will you go? You haven't been on a holiday since I don't know when.'

'Which is why I'm going now,' Aunt Elsie

said. 'I've booked myself a few days in the Outer Hebrides—on the Isle of Harris to start with. I've an old pen-pal from school who lives there. Her husband passed away recently so she could do with some company. You'll be right with looking after Flossie for a few days?'

'Of course,' Logan said. 'We're not going anywhere.'

That was news to Layla. What about his big landscaping project in Tuscany that he'd put on hold? Surely he couldn't postpone it too much longer. She had expected him to deliver her back to Bellbrae and fly out again as soon as he could to put even more distance between them. Had he changed his mind? And if so, why?

'Do you need transport? A lift anywhere?' Logan continued.

'Och, no, I've got it all sorted,' Aunt Elsie said. 'I'm being picked up in half an hour by my friend's daughter. I thought that was her just now but I saw it was Robbie. He didn't stay?'

'No,' Logan said, his mouth pulled into a grim line. 'He had other plans.'

'Good.' Aunt Elsie smiled as if she'd just received the best news of the day. 'You'll be all alone.'

Logan left Layla to say her goodbyes to her great-aunt and saw to some business in his grandfather's study. It was strange to think of it now as *his* study. Strange but deeply satisfying. He cast his gaze around the room, from the wall-to-wall bookshelves, the leather-topped desk that both his father and grandfather had used, at the Aubusson carpet that generations of McLaughlins had walked on. He looked out of the windows that overlooked the estate—the loch, the forest, the Highlands that were currently shrouded by clouds.

The whole of Bellbrae now belonged to him, thanks to Layla's willingness to be his bride. His *paper* bride. He had to keep reminding himself of that simple fact. Not so simple when she made him feel things he didn't want to feel. Things he had forbidden himself to feel. He had been so close to kissing her before her great-aunt had interrupted them. So close to once again disregarding the rules he had set down. The rules he was having trouble obeying because of the aching need their lovemaking had awakened.

By making love with her, he had crossed a threshold and he couldn't find a way back. The door had slammed behind him and no matter how hard he tried to prise it open, it wouldn't budge. His body had been reprogrammed, finely tuned to notice every one of her movements, to respond to every smile or velvet-like touch.

He suppressed a whole-body tremor. It was her touch he craved. The glide of her small hands over his flesh, the press of her soft lips to his mouth, the playful teasing of her tongue, the hot wet tight cocoon of her body.

He wanted it all, hungered for it like he would starve without it. It consumed him like a fever, it occupied his every thought, it kept him from sleep.

Logan walked back to the desk and sent the leather chair into a slow spin, his forehead tight with a frown. He had planned to fly to Italy to check in on his project but he didn't feel comfortable leaving Layla alone now her great-aunt wouldn't be at Bellbrae. There were ground staff who came and went on the estate but the castle was a big place to stay in alone. And these days Flossie was hardly what anyone could describe as a guard dog.

There was a tap at the door. 'Logan?' Layla's voice called out.

'Come in.'

She opened the door and entered the study with the old dog padding slowly behind her. She had changed from her travelling outfit into black leggings and an oversized dove-grey boyfriend sweater that had slipped off one creamy shoulder, revealing the thin white strap of her bra. 'Am I interrupting you?'

'No.' He walked from behind the desk and bent down to scratch Flossie behind the ears. He glanced up at Layla. 'What's up?'

She hitched her sweater back over her shoulder. 'I was wondering what you wanted me to do about…um…our sleeping arrangements.' Her cheeks were stained a faint shade of pink. 'Now that Aunt Elsie is going away and Robbie's not around, we don't have to share the west tower suite. For appearances' sake, I mean.'

Logan rose to his full height, only just resisting the urge to put his arms around her and draw her closer. She licked her lower lip and a lightning bolt of lust zapped him in the groin. 'Are you worried I might not stick to the rules?' he asked. Damn it. *He* was worried. Right at that moment he couldn't think of a single reason why he should stick to the rules.

Her gaze skittered away from his, concentrating on the open neck of his shirt instead. She began to pluck at the overly long sleeve of her sweater as if she needed something to do with her hands. 'No, of course not. I just thought you'd prefer it if I was in my own quarters. Away from you. Or at least, that's the message I've been getting since we left Hawaii.'

Logan inched up her chin with the end of his finger, meshing his gaze with hers. Every rational cell in his body told him to stop. Do not pass go. Do not go any further. But right then his body was programmed to follow instinct, not rationality. A primal instinct that demanded contact. Physical contact.

Intimate contact.

'The problem is, I don't want you away from me.' He slid a hand behind her head to the nape of her neck under the silky curtain of her hair. 'I want you close to me. Closer than is probably wise.' He breathed in the fresh flowery scent of her perfume, his senses going haywire, his blood thickening with each thunderous beat of his pulse.

She closed her eyes in a slow blink, like a sensuous cat enjoying a caress. Her lips softly parting, her breath hitching, her slim throat rising and falling over a swallow. 'Why is that a problem when I want the same thing?' Her voice was husky and it sent another punch of lust into his lower body.

Logan slowly brought his mouth down to hers, promising himself one taste, one reminder of how sweet and soft her lips were. But as soon as their lips met, a wave of intense heat swept through him and he deepened the kiss with a gliding thrust of his tongue that made her moan and press herself closer. His arms went around her, holding her to the length of his hardening body, desire hot and strong rippling through him in an unstoppable tide.

He buried one hand in the thick tresses of her hair, the other pressed into the small of her back to keep her pressed against him, his mouth locked on hers in a kiss that sent shivers across his scalp and down the entire length of his spine. He lifted his mouth off hers to graze her neck with his teeth, breathing in the scent of her skin. 'I can't tell you how hard I've fought with myself not to do this.'

'But I want you to do it.' Layla moved against

him, sending a whiplash of longing through his body. 'I want you.'

'I want you so much it's driving me nuts.' He groaned and clamped his mouth back down on hers, their lips moving in perfect motion as if they had been kissing for years. Her tongue touched his and the backs of his knees tingled, his blood pounding through his veins like a tribal drum.

He lifted her sweater so he could access her breasts, desperate to feel her soft creamy skin against his palm. He unclipped her bra to find her nipples were already tightly budded and he lowered his mouth to each one in turn, lavishing them with strokes and licks of his tongue, teasing them with the gentle press of his teeth. She made soft murmurs of approval, her breathing rate increasing, her hands reaching for the waistband of his trousers.

Logan hauled her sweater over her head, tossing it to the floor and only just missing Flossie, who was lying on her side, snoring. It was enough to break his stride and he took a deep steadying breath and grasped Layla by the upper arms. 'Let's take this upstairs. I want you to be comfortable and I'd rather not have an audience.' He jerked his head towards the sleeping dog.

A shadow of worry passed through Layla's gaze. 'What if you change your mind before we get upstairs? I thought you were okay with taking our relationship further the other night but then you seemed to change your mind and could barely look at me, much less talk to me.'

He took one of her hands and brought it up to his mouth, pressing a kiss to the backs of her knuckles, his eyes locked on hers. 'If I was a better man—a stronger man—then that's exactly what I would do. I would reinstate the rules. But apparently I'm not as strong as I thought.' He released her hand and bent down to retrieve her sweater, helping her put it back on like she was a small child.

She smiled as her head came out of the top of the sweater and something near his heart split open, leaking warmth into every cold and closed-off cavity of his chest. His breath hitched, his heart stuttered, his desire throbbed and pounded. He had never wanted anyone with such fervour, with such ferocity, with such frightening intensity. It was a clawing need inside him that he was worried would get out of control. Making him want her longer than the year they had agreed on. Making him want things he had sworn he would never want again. Closeness, commitment, connection beyond the physical. A lasting connection that would only get deeper, more abiding and bonding each and every year.

But it was a risk he was prepared to take because he couldn't go another day—another moment—without experiencing the heart-stopping thrill of their intimate union.

Logan framed her face in his hands, lowering his mouth to hers in a lingering kiss, closing down his conscience, shutting away his fears, slamming the door on his damn rules.

He wanted her.

She wanted him.

That's all that mattered for now.

Their journey to Logan's room upstairs was a stop-start affair with kisses and caresses at various points along the way. Finally, they made it to the bed and he laid Layla down and leaned over her, kissing her lingeringly with his hands propped either side of her head, one of his knees resting on the bed near her legs. He raised his head to look down at her. 'I can't tell you how much I want you,' he said, breathing as heavily as her.

'Then don't tell me. Show me.' Layla wound her arms around his neck and brought his head back down so his mouth met hers.

His kiss was deep and thrilling, his tongue dancing with hers in a sexy salsa that made her spine loosen vertebra by vertebra. Her heart picked up its pace, her pulse pounding with the need to have him closer, to feel him skin on skin.

He lifted his mouth off hers to blaze a fiery trail of kisses along the sensitive skin of her neck, down lower to the shallow dish between her collarbones. She shivered in reaction, tingling from head to foot as desire swept through her in hot spreading waves. How could she have spent so many years of her life without experiencing this incredible passion? How could she experience it with anyone else? He was the one who evoked such powerful responses from her. Responses that travelled through her body with the force of a tumultuous storm. A tornado of lust that left her senses spinning in its wake.

Logan helped her out of her clothes and she did the same for him, but with nowhere near the same efficiency. Her fingers fumbled in her haste and he eventually took over the task and stripped off the last of his clothes. He applied a condom and came back down on the bed beside her, gliding his hands over her naked breasts, and her spine arched when his mouth came down to kiss around her achingly tight nipple. Layla made a moaning sound as pleasure shot through her. A dragging ache tugged deep and low in her womanhood—a need that begged to be assuaged.

He took her nipple into his mouth, his lips and tongue caressing it with such exquisite expertise she whimpered and writhed, impatient, greedy, desperate for more. He kissed the gentle slopes of each breast, paying particular attention to the sensitive undersides. She was almost breathless with excitement when his teeth softly grazed each nipple in turn, and her hips rose against him in a wordless plea for him to tame the raging desire barrelling through her body.

'I'll take things slowly. I don't want to hurt you again.' His voice was deep and low and husky.

Layla stroked her finger along the contour of his bottom lip. 'You didn't hurt me the first time and I don't want you to go slowly. I need you inside me.' She placed her hands on his buttocks and pushed him down towards her.

He drew in a sharp breath and entered her slickly, visibly fighting for control, his features contorted in a mixture of agony and ecstasy. He began to move with gentle thrusts, each one getting deeper and deeper until he was up to the hilt.

He gave a guttural groan and increased his pace and Layla was with him all the way, swept up in the primal rhythm that made her flesh sing. The need spiralled through every part of her body, building to a crescendo.

She hovered at the edge, needing more, straining to reach the final tipping point but not quite able to get there. She whimpered and moved her body against his, desperately seeking more friction. But then his hand slipped down between their rocking bodies to touch her, sending her over the edge into the throes of a powerful orgasm, intensified by his continued thrusting. She shattered into a thousand pieces, her body racked by tingling waves of sensation that went on and on and on, finally leaving her spent and limbless and breath-less in his arms.

His release followed on the tail of hers and she drew vicarious pleasure from holding him through each shuddering thrust, riding out the storm with him as he tensed at the point of no return and then finally let go.

Logan lifted his head and, leaning his weight on his elbows, pressed a soft kiss to her mouth. His expression was bathed in lines of relaxation, his gaze warm and heart-stoppingly tender.

'No regrets?' His tone was low as a bass chord and it sent a tingly shiver cascading down her spine.

'None from me,' Layla said, tracing his upper lip with her finger. 'You?'

He took her finger into his mouth and sucked on it, his gaze glinting. He released her finger and tucked a strand of hair behind her ear, his mouth twisting into a rueful line. 'No. Not one. It was— *you were*—wonderful.'

Layla stroked her hand along his jaw from below his ear to the base of his chin. 'Thank you for making it so good for me. I feel so at ease with you. I can't explain why other than you seem to read my body like it's an extension of your own. How do you *do* that?'

He gave a lopsided smile and leaned down to kiss the tip of her nose. 'It doesn't happen often but sometimes it just works from the start with some partners. The chemistry is right.' He rolled away to dispose of the condom and came back to lie beside her with his elbow bent, his head propped against his hand. His other hand began a lazy journey from her breast to her thigh and back again. Slow, sensual, setting her flesh alight all over again.

Layla rolled towards him, her mouth meeting his in a scorching kiss that sent a hot wave of need shooting through her body. Her legs entwined with his, the roughness of his sending another shiver coursing down her spine. He took a handful of her hair and bunched it against her scalp, his kiss deepening, his tongue playing, teasing, tangling with hers.

He dragged his mouth away and gazed down at her with a rueful expression. 'I'd better stop before I can't stop. You need to get used to this gradually otherwise you could get sore.'

His tender consideration towards her was so touching it made her breath catch. She stroked his jaw again, raising her head to brush his lips with hers. 'You've created a bit of an addiction in me. I don't want to wait. I want you again…but is it too soon for you?'

He gave a low deep laugh and rolled her beneath him, his eyes dark and gleaming with lust. 'What do you think?' And then his mouth came down on hers and she stopped thinking altogether.

CHAPTER TEN

LOGAN HAD MOSTLY travelled abroad during the month of November, so he could escape the all too often grey and dismal progression of the Highlands' final month of autumn into winter. But spending the time with Layla at Bellbrae had turned the normally cold and bleak time into something else entirely. The shorter days and longer nights were no longer an inconvenience but an excellent excuse to relax over a drink in front of a roaring fire. Or to spend long hours in bed, making love, then snuggling up in a cocoon of cosy warmth. And with winter and plenty of snowbound days heading their way, instead of feeling trapped and contained, he felt... *free.*

More open, more relaxed. More human and less of an emotionless workhorse machine.

The days at Bellbrae belonged to Layla and him, no one else. Well, apart from Flossie but the old dog spent most of the time snoozing by the fire, only stirring for meals and comfort breaks. Aunt

Elsie had extended her holiday and, apart from the occasional ground staff going about their business on the estate, Logan and Layla were entirely, blissfully alone.

They each juggled their work commitments but he was increasingly worried about monopolising her time. Her generous and giving nature often had her putting her needs aside for others'. Hadn't her closing her Edinburgh office when his grandfather had gone into his final decline been proof of that? He knew he should be encouraging her to find another office off site but he couldn't bring himself to do it. He was enjoying their time together too much. He had even put another delay on his visit to Tuscany to check the progress on his project. It was out of character for him but he had competent people working for him and knew they would call him instantly if there was anything that only he could fix.

Logan left Layla sleeping while he rose early to let Flossie out downstairs. He slipped on track-suit bottoms and slip-on shoes in case the old dog went further into the garden and got disoriented in the darkness. It had happened before and it had taken him half an hour to find her—not ideal in only boxers or less and bare feet.

The sun wasn't up yet and the frost was as thick as a carpet on the ground, the air so cold it burned his face. An owl hooted from a nearby tree and then Logan heard the swish of its wings as the bird flew off into the misty darkness. The distinctive call of a vixen looking for a mate would once have made Flossie's ears prick and her tail rise, but the old dog barely seemed to notice. She squatted on a frosty patch of ground and sighed with relief and then came plodding back to where Logan was standing, her feathery tail wagging back and forth.

'Good girl.' He bent down and ruffled her ears. 'Back to bed for you, hey?'

'Sounds good to me,' Layla's voice sounded from behind him. 'Gosh, it's freezing, isn't it?'

Logan turned, saw her framed in the doorway and something in his chest slipped. Funny, but he didn't feel cold at all. He felt warm. Hot. Hotter than hot—for her. She was dressed in his bathrobe, which was far too big for her. It swamped her petite frame and made her look like a child who had been playing with a dress-up box.

'I was about to wake you up with a cup of tea,' he said with a smile.

She rubbed her crossed-over hands up and down her arms and shivered but a smile played about her mouth. And her eyes contained a light that made his lower body sit up and take notice. 'Stop spoiling me. I'll be hell to live with if you keep treating me like a princess.'

'I'll take the risk.' He came over to her and leaned down to drop a kiss to the end of her upturned nose and then led her back inside to the warmth of the castle kitchen.

Thing was, she wasn't hell to live with. She was heaven. He had only lived with one other lover— his late fiancée—and it had definitely not been anything like this. His time with Layla worked so seamlessly, so easily, so naturally. He didn't have to second-guess or play games or have games played on him. Layla was a complex person but not a difficult one. He could relax around her, be more open and share things he hadn't shared with anyone before.

There was a growing part of him that didn't want their 'married fling' to end, which was a deeply troubling thought. The locked no long-term-commitment vault inside his mind had some-how allowed a sliver of light in under the door. A beam of light he wasn't sure he wanted illumi-nating the darkly shadowed corners of his mind.

One month had already passed on their one-year marriage. It was ticking away like a clock set on fast forward. Christmas would be here soon, then Hogmanay and then before he knew it, the year would be up.

Their marriage would come to its inevitable end. The end he had insisted on. That he *still* in-sisted on—didn't he?

So why did that seem far more of a problem than it had before?

* * *

They were in the kitchen, waiting for the kettle to boil on the stove, and Layla put her arms around his waist and rested her head on his chest. 'What do you have planned for today?'

He tipped up her face with his hand so she was looking up at him. 'You mean apart from going back to bed and making mad passionate love to you and then serving you breakfast in bed, and after that showering together?' His eyes were glinting and his lower body already stirring against her.

Layla lifted her hand to his stubbly jaw, tracing the line of his smiling mouth with her fingertip, her insides twisting and coiling with desire. 'I don't think I've ever spent so much time in bed before, not even when I've been sick.'

'Neither have I.' His voice had a husky quality that made her feel weak at the knees.

He lowered his head and covered her mouth with his in a kiss that made the ache inside her body go to fever pitch. His hands went to the small of her back, drawing her closer to his body—closer to the potency of his erection. His tongue played with hers in an erotic dance that made something swoop and dive in her belly. His mouth moved from her lips to the side of her neck, his tongue leaving a hot trail along her sensitive flesh. He used his teeth to gently nip her earlobe and a shiver shot down her spine at rocket speed.

He pulled apart the dark blue bathrobe she was wearing and uncovered her naked breasts. He caressed each breast with his lips and tongue until her inner core was melting and flowing like scorching-hot lava. His teeth grazed her nipple, his tongue rolling over its tight point, and desire drummed a primitive beat between her legs.

'Why didn't I think to leave a supply of condoms in every room?' he said, with a rueful grin.

Layla rummaged in the pocket of the bathrobe, which was hanging around her hips with just the waist tie keeping it in place. She took out a tiny foil packet and handed it to him.

He took the condom from her, his eyes darkening to a glittering blue-black. 'I just love your organisational and planning skills. You really do think of everything.'

'Glad to be of service.'

A shadow flickered across his face and he drew in a breath and pulled the edges of the bathrobe back around her shoulders, slipping the condom back in the pocket. 'Layla.' There was a guarded quality to his voice, his expression losing its earlier teasing playfulness and changing into a frown.

A cold ghost hand pressed against the back of her neck, sending a flow of ice over her scalp. 'What's wrong? What did I say to make you frown at me like that?' It had been a flippant comment, sure, but why had it upset him so much?

Logan let out a long breath. 'I don't want you to feel like you're just here to service my needs. It's important to me that you feel equal in our relationship.'

Did she feel it was an equal relationship? In some ways, yes. In others, no. How could it be truly equal when he was the one who insisted their marriage end at a specific point? 'It was just a throwaway line. I didn't mean anything by it.'

'This past month has been good, better than good, but it's not always going to be like this,' he said, still frowning in a brooding manner. 'We can't live in a bubble at Bellbrae for ever. You have work commitments and so do I.'

Now it was Layla's turn to frown, her mood soured by the sudden change in his. 'Have I stopped you from doing your work? I haven't exactly chained you to my side. You're perfectly free to fly off to wherever you need to, whenever you need to.' She spun away to lift the whistling kettle off the hob and place it on a heat protector, all but steaming herself. Why did he have to remind her this last month together wasn't going to last? She didn't need reminding. It was front and centre in her head every single day.

'I don't want to argue with—' he began.

'Then stop blaming me for you feeling guilty about taking time off,' Layla shot back, turning to face him. 'You're a human being, Logan, not a flipping robot.'

He moved across the floor to place his hands on the tops of her shoulders, giving them a light squeeze. His eyes were troubled, his frown still in place. 'But what about your work? I'm concerned you haven't got an office away from here yet.'

Layla pulled out of his hold and folded her arms across her body, her glower hotter than the hotplate the kettle had just come off. 'Oh, so that's what this is about? You're worried I'm going to get too comfortable working from here once the time is up on our marriage? Well, here's some news for you. I've already been looking online at potential rentals in Edinburgh. There's one in the Old Town that looks promising. It's a bit expensive but I want the position to attract good clientele. It's got a tiny bedsit upstairs so I can stay there if I don't feel up to driving back here. And I can live there once our marriage ends.'

His frown deepened. 'You're surely not thinking of commuting between here and Edinburgh over the winter? The roads are treacherous with black ice and snow and—'

'Make up your mind, Logan,' Layla mock-laughed. 'You either want me to prioritise my work over you or you don't.'

He came back to her and placed his hands on her hips, pulling her back against him. 'That's the whole damn problem.' His tone was a low rumbling growl, his expression still set in brooding lines. 'I don't want to share you with your work or with anyone and it scares the hell out of me.' And then his mouth came down heavily, explosively on hers.

It was a kiss of lust and anger and frustration and scorching need racing out of control. But she relished every heart-stopping second of it. His mouth was a fire on hers, his tongue a flame teasing hers into a combative dance with bone-melting expertise.

Layla thought her legs were folding beneath her but he had picked her up and sat her on the kitchen bench in front of him. Her legs parted and he stepped between her open thighs, his mouth still locked on hers. The closeness of his erection, the molten heat building in her body, the escalating need communicated by their mouths was a potent combination.

Logan untied the waistband of the bathrobe and stripped it off her shoulders, leaving her naked and exposed to his smouldering gaze. His eyes travelled over her breasts, his hands cradling them before placing his mouth on each in turn, subjecting them to a spine-tingling array of licks and strokes and circles of his tongue. Darts of pleasure shot through her and she shuffled as close to him as she possibly could.

Logan rummaged in the pocket of her discarded bathrobe for the condom, swiftly tugging down his trousers and applying it. He surged into her with a primal groan of satisfaction, thrusting deeply and rhythmically, making her senses spin out of control. The delicious pressure built and built to bursting point and then, with the added caress of his fingers against her most sensitive female flesh, she was tossed into the maelstrom of a powerful orgasm. She cried, she gasped, she shook, she shuddered and quaked and still it went on in ripples and waves that were only intensified by his release, which coincided with hers.

Logan framed her face in his hands, his breathing still laboured. 'I've always wanted to do that.'

Layla brushed his hair back from his forehead, gazing into his intensely blue eyes. 'Do what? Kitchen bench sex?'

His mouth tilted in a crooked smile. 'Yeah.' He brushed her lips with his and added, 'I was a kitchen bench sex virgin. You're so damn hot I can barely keep control of myself no matter what room we're in.'

His words thrilled her as much as his red-hot passion had moments earlier. She pressed her lips against his, once, twice, three times, pulling back to meet his gaze. 'What you said before… About it scaring you how much you want to spend time with me? I feel like that too.' Her voice was as soft as a whisper and for a moment she wondered if he'd even heard.

Flickers of deliberation passed through his gaze—thoughts and considerations, worries and balances being carefully weighed. 'We don't have to think too far ahead, sweetheart.' His tone was as rusty as the lych-gate hinge in the garden. 'We can just enjoy what we have for now.'

For now.

Layla wanted more than 'for now', but how could she be sure she would get it?

Later that evening, Logan put some more wood on the fire and then came back to sit with Layla on the sofa. She was dressed in a baby-blue cashmere sweater and black yoga pants that clung to her shapely legs like a velvet evening glove. Her hair was in a loosely tied knot at the back of her head, highlighting her finely boned features and elegant neck. He had always considered her beautiful, but lately he couldn't look at her without his breathing catching and a warm flow of heat spreading in his chest.

Layla looked up from the magazine she was idly flicking through. 'It will soon be time to put up the Christmas tree. Will you get a real one from the forest like before or a fake one?'

'It wouldn't be Christmas without the smell of pine needles,' Logan said, playing with a loose curl dangling below her ear. But, then, it wouldn't be Christmas without her bustling about the castle, helping her great-aunt get ready for the festive season. It wouldn't be Christmas without the delicious cooking smells coming from the kitchen. So many of his memories had snapshots of Layla in them. She had become an essential part of Bellbrae and he couldn't imagine the place without her. And—even more disturbing to his carefully guarded emotions—he couldn't imagine his life without her.

'True.' Layla closed the magazine and leaned forward to put it on the coffee table in front of the sofa. She sat back next to him, her gaze meeting his. 'But will you invite anyone? Will Robbie come home for it, do you think?'

'I have no idea what his plans are,' Logan said with an all-too-familiar knot of tension in his stomach whenever his younger brother was mentioned. 'You know what he's like—he'll just show up unannounced and expect everyone to dance around him like some overgrown overly indulged teenager.' He leaned his head back against the back of the sofa and released a frustrated sigh. 'I wish I could go back in time and do things differently. I thought I was doing the right thing by being easy on him but…' He left the sentence hanging with all the unspoken things he wished now he had done.

'You did what you thought was right at the time,' Layla said. 'We all have a PhD in hindsight. I think he'll wake up to himself one day. He's just taking a little longer than you hoped.'

Logan took her hand and brought it up to rest on his thigh. 'I can't help comparing you to him. Unlike Robbie, you weren't born to privilege. You've had such a rough time of it and yet you're a kind and compassionate person who is always giving your time and attention to others. I feel ashamed that Robbie hasn't made the most of the opportunities he's been given. Deeply ashamed and frustrated. He could have done so much more with his life but he's throwing it away, along with the trust fund our father left him.'

He sighed again and added in a weighted tone, 'I feel like I've failed Robbie *and* my father. That I've let them both down. And the guilt that comes with that churns my guts.'

Layla touched his face with the soft palm of her hand, her expression full of concern. 'Oh, Logan, you really mustn't blame yourself for how Robbie chooses to live his life. You and Robbie have had terrible tragedy in your lives. It must have been awful to have your mother walk out like that when you were both so young. But she didn't just walk out on Robbie and your father. She abandoned you as well. But it seems like you've had to be strong for everyone else. And then when your dad died… well, you did the same. It's in your nature to take control, to make sure everyone is okay before you see to your own needs. But your needs are important too. You can't put them on hold for ever.'

Logan cradled one side of her face with his hand, his other hand still holding her hand anchored to his thigh. 'How'd you get to be so wise and wonderful?'

Something passed through her gaze and she lowered her eyes to focus on the region of his collar. 'I'm not that wonderful…' She bit her lip and a frown pleated her smooth brow.

He lifted her chin so her gaze came back to his. 'Hey. Why do you think that?'

Her expression faltered as if she was in two minds over answering. But then she gave a jagged sigh and spoke in a muted and flat tone. 'When my parents died in the car crash… I didn't grieve for them. Not the way other kids would have grieved. I pretended to grieve, because that's what everyone expected. But I was a fraud because I was secretly relieved I didn't have to live that chaotic life with them anymore.'

Her mouth tightened as if the memories were almost too painful to speak out loud.

'The drugs, the drink binges, the violence— I hated my life and I hated being first-row witness to what my mother's life had become. But I couldn't do anything to make it better for her. But the "accident—"' she did the air quote gesture with her fingers '—changed my life for ever and I was *glad*. I was actually more relieved I didn't have to have my leg amputated than I grieved for my parents. How sick and screwed up is that? I think that makes me a bad person. A terrible person.'

Logan hugged her tightly against his chest, resting his chin on the top of her head. 'You're not any such thing, sweetheart. You were a neglected and maltreated little girl who deserved a much better start in life. My heart aches for what you went through. But you should be proud of how you've coped. For what you've done with your life.' He eased back to blot the tears from beneath her eyes with his thumbs. 'What you're doing for others in your mother's situation is a wonderful way of breaking the cycle. It's your legacy for her memory and I'm sure she would be so very proud of you.'

Her lips flickered with a wry smile. 'Gosh, this sofa has become confession central lately, hasn't it? What is it about a roaring fire and a cosy atmosphere that gets under one's guard?'

It hadn't just lowered her guard—Logan had never been so open with anyone before. It was a strange feeling—a feeling he wasn't sure he could or wanted to name. He framed her face in his hands and brought his lips within a breath of hers. 'I don't know but it sure feels pretty damn good.' And he covered her mouth with his.

CHAPTER ELEVEN

PREPARING FOR CHRISTMAS at Bellbrae had always been one of Layla's favourite pastimes, but with Logan there to offer his assistance, it took her enjoyment to a whole new level. He helped her select a tree from the forest on the estate and with two of the grounds staff's help, it was transported to the largest sitting room in the castle.

In the past, Layla and her great-aunt had done the decorating of the tree, especially in later years when Logan and his brother had often been abroad and Logan's grandfather had been too infirm to do much more than sit and watch and offer suggestions about where a bauble or strip of tinsel should be placed.

They were in the sitting room, putting the last touches to the tree, Logan standing on a ladder while she held it steady so he could place the porcelain angel, which had been in the McLaughlin family for six decades, at the top of the tree.

'There,' he said with a note of satisfaction in his voice. 'Let's hope she makes it through one more festive season, but I seriously think we might have to get a new one for next year.' He climbed down the ladder and began tidying up the boxes in which the decorations had been stored.

Next year? Layla mentally gulped. *We?*

There would be no 'we' next year. Their marriage would have ended in October, as Logan had planned from the start. Or would it? He had been so wonderful to her over the last few weeks. Attentive and loving…yes, *loving.* Surely it wasn't just an act? There was nobody around to witness it, as Aunt Elsie had extended her holiday, and the other Bellbrae staff were mostly casual and weren't in the castle much but working in the outbuildings or grounds.

Logan turned with two empty boxes in his arms and frowned at her expression. 'Hey, what's wrong, sweetie?'

'Nothing…' Layla bent down to pick up a tiny strip of silver tinsel off the carpet.

He put the boxes down and came over to where she was standing and brushed his finger across her lower lip. 'If you keep chewing your lip like that it will bleed and then I won't be able to kiss you.'

Layla forced a quick no-teeth smile. 'I guess I'm just a bit tired…'

He tucked a loose strand of her hair behind her

ear, his gaze so dark it was hard to tell where his pupils began and ended. 'Is your leg hurting you? You've been doing way too much and that walk to the forest to get the tree was a bit rough in places.'

'My leg is okay, mostly,' Layla said. The chronic neural pain she suffered from was still there but she was less conscious of it. She still limped, because one leg was shorter than the other, but she realised she had become almost oblivious to the slight awkwardness of her gait. 'I think you've helped distract me from the discomfort.' She put her arms around his waist and smiled, properly this time. 'Now, we need to find some mistletoe to hang over the doorway.'

Logan's eyes twinkled. 'Who needs mistletoe?' He lowered his mouth to hers in a long drugging kiss that made Layla's senses sing. It was silly of her to keep filling her head with doubts over the future. Silly of her to listen to alarm bells ringing in her head…except they weren't in her head.

Logan lifted his mouth off hers and cocked his head. 'Is that your phone or mine?'

'Mine.' Layla slipped out of his loose hold and picked up her phone from one of the lamp tables where she'd left it earlier. She glanced at the caller ID and smiled and answered the phone. 'Hi, Isla. How are you? I was going to call you and—'

'Guess what?' Excitement and joy sounded in Isla's voice.

Layla's heart skipped a beat 'Oh, my God, you've had the baby?'

'Yes, a little girl,' Isla said. 'She was in a big hurry to get here—almost three weeks early—and I was only in labour two hours. Rafe was beside himself, trying to get me to the hospital in time. We've called her Gabriella Marietta Layla. I can't wait for you to meet her. She's adorable. Rafe is completely and utterly smitten.'

Tears came to Layla's eyes and her chest swelled with love for her friend. 'You named her after me? Oh, my goodness, I don't know what to say.'

'Say you'll be her godmother,' Isla said. 'And we'd like Logan to be her godfather. We would be so honoured to have you both as Gabriella's godparents.'

Layla pictured Logan standing with her at the christening font, agreeing to spiritually sponsor their godchild. It was such an honour for any couple. And since they had become more of a connected couple than before, it seemed the perfect cementing of their relationship. Didn't their increasing closeness signify a more promising future together? There were times when she was almost certain he loved her. He hadn't said it but his body, his gaze, his touch said it for him. And didn't hers tell him much the same?

'We would be delighted to,' Layla said. 'I can't

wait to meet her in person. Can you put the face camera feature on so I can see her now?'

'Here we go…' Isla did the necessary button-pressing and the real-time camera showed a tiny pink bundle cradled in her adoring father's arms.

Layla was so overcome with emotion once she got off the phone that she could barely speak. Happy joyful emotion. Jubilation for her friend and for the love and security she had found in Rafe. That was what she wanted with Logan. Lasting love, a family. Building a harmonious home life together. 'Gosh, I can't believe I'm a sort of aunty. And a godmother.' She turned to Logan and smiled. 'Did you hear? We've been invited to be Gabriella's godparents. I've never been a godparent before, have you?'

Logan's expression and posture were so still he could have been snap-frozen while she'd been on the phone. 'No. I have not.' His voice was flat, almost toneless, except for a fine thread of anger running underneath.

Layla frowned, her heart missing a beat. Why was he looking so cold and distant? 'What's wrong?'

He drew in a sharp breath and moved a few paces away, released the breath and then turned back to face her. 'Do you not think it might have been appropriate to ask me first before accepting an invitation like that?'

Layla swallowed a bauble-sized lump in her throat. 'But I thought you'd be honoured to—'

'You thought wrong,' he said, brows drawn down heavily in a brooding frown.

'Logan...' She tried for a conciliatory tone but missed the mark. 'Why are you so upset? Being asked to be a godparent is such a lovely thing. It's mostly symbolic these days but, still, it's wonderful to be asked. I would feel awful saying no. And besides, they want both of us.'

'You've seen the rubbish job I've done of being responsible for my brother. And don't get me started on what a mess I made with Susannah. I'm not signing up for any more responsibility, especially when we're not really a couple. Or at least not for the long term.'

Not really a couple. Not for the long term.

The words hit her like slaps. Cold hard stinging slaps of truth. A truth she had been hiding from for weeks and weeks, fooling herself her relationship with Logan was something else. Something like Isla had with Rafe. But it wasn't. It never had been and never could be.

Why had she fooled herself it could?

Layla took a steadying breath, trying to control her spiralling emotions. 'So, what you're saying is you don't want to be Gabriella's godfather?'

'I don't want to be any child's godfather.' His eyes were as hard as his tone. Diamond hard.

Don't-ask-me-twice hard. 'You had no right to answer for me. We might be having a good time but it doesn't mean you get to sign me up for things I have no interest in.'

'A good time?' Layla gasped. 'Is that all this is to you? Is that all *I* am to you?' Pain ripped through her chest as if her ribcage was being wrenched apart with steel claws. But she wouldn't allow herself to cry. Not now. Not in front of him. How could she have been so gullible, so foolish as to think their physical closeness meant emotional closeness? He was as far away from her as he had ever been. She had fooled herself that his touch meant he loved her. That his passionate kisses meant he cared. That his lovemaking was *lovemaking*, not just sex.

Logan shoved his hands into his trouser pockets, glaring at her like she was an intruder he had never seen before and not the woman he had spent the last two months making passionate love to. 'Don't put words in my mouth. I told you right at the start how things were going to be. You accepted my terms.'

'Your terms are completely ridiculous,' Layla said. 'They're your insurance scheme against getting hurt, that's what they really are. And here I was thinking my limp was holding me back, stopping me doing all the things other people do. But at the end of the day it's just a physical limp. Your emotional limp is far worse. It completely disables you and yet you can't see it.'

He gave a mocking laugh that grated on her already shredded emotions. 'Thanks for the free psychoanalysis but I don't need you to tell me how I think.'

'You don't need me at all,' Layla said. 'You don't need anyone. You won't allow yourself to. Which is why I can't stay here any longer. I can't be in a relationship that has limits set on it. I spent my childhood trying to fit in with impossible standards. Standards that didn't factor in my needs or aspirations. Standards that didn't include love. I want more than that now. I deserve more than that and you do too.'

His expression was masked but she sensed a simmering anger behind the dark screen of his gaze. 'You're free to come and go as you please. I can't make you stay.'

Yes, you can, Layla wanted to say. *Just three little words would make me stay.*

But those three little words had never been a part of their arrangement. Neither had a future together ever been part of the deal. Logan had always been blatantly honest about that. 'I don't think it will help either of us if I were to stay on in this relationship. Of course, I won't jeopardise your inheritance of Bellbrae. I will be your wife on paper, as you first suggested, to fulfil the terms of your grandfather's will.'

'Magnanimous of you.' His coolly delivered comment was as cutting as a switchblade.

Layla pressed her lips together to stop them from trembling. She couldn't fall apart now. He was making it perfectly clear there was no hope for their marriage. No hope at all. 'I think it's best if I leave straight away. I will pack a few things and come for the rest later.'

'There's no need to be so dramatic, Layla,' Logan said. 'I'm sure we can be perfectly civil to each other until tomorrow morning. It'll be dark in a couple of hours. I don't like the thought of you driving all the way to Edinburgh at this time of day.'

And risk having him try and change her mind? No. It was better she leave now while she still had the strength and courage and self-respect to do so. Layla raised her chin to a determined height, her gaze steady on his unreadable one. 'I appreciate your concern, but my mind is made up.'

Anger flared in his gaze and his mouth went into a flat line and he began a caged-tiger-like pacing of the floor. 'This all seems rather sudden and impulsive.' He stopped pacing to spear her with a look. 'A few minutes ago, we were kissing. Now you say you want out?'

Layla smoothed her sweaty palms down her

thighs, wishing she could smooth away the heartache she was feeling. 'It's not as sudden as you might think. I've been worried from the start—you know I have. I didn't want you to lose Bellbrae. But I can't lose myself in the process of you gaining your inheritance. And that's what's already happening. I can't be who I'm meant to be if I'm tailoring my needs to suit your plans. I have my own plans and they don't include a short-term loveless marriage.'

He rolled his eyes heavenwards and let out a not-quite-inaudible curse. 'Oh, I thought you'd mention the L word eventually. You think I don't care about you? Is that what you think?'

Layla forced herself to hold his embittered gaze. 'I know you care. You care about lots of people. But you don't love me.'

He sucked in a harsh breath and strode to stand in front of the waist-height bookcase. 'You're suddenly such an expert on my feelings.' He pushed a hand through his hair and then dropped it back by his side. 'Love?' He shook his head and let out another breath and continued, 'I don't trust that emotion. I don't trust the word when people say it to me. My mother said it so frequently and look how that turned out.' His gaze narrowed. 'Are you saying you love me?'

Layla ran the tip of her tongue over her parchment-dry lips. 'It wouldn't matter if I did or not. You don't love me the way I want to be loved.'

He closed his eyes and pinched the bridge of his nose. After a moment, he lowered his hand from his face to look at her. 'No one can love anyone the way they want to be loved. The standard is set too high, fed by romantic fantasies encouraged by popular culture. It's not real, Layla. What you feel for me is not real, it's just a fantasy.'

How like him to intellectualise everything. How like him to dismiss her feelings as simple fantasy. What hope was there to ever change his mind? She had seen her mother try desperately to get her father to love her and it hadn't happened. Layla had tried to get both her parents to love her and yet the drugs and drink had triumphed over her. Lucky Layla wasn't so lucky after all.

She was unlucky in love.

'I'm going upstairs to pack. I'll text you when I arrive in Edinburgh.'

'Fine.'

Layla took off the engagement ring and held it out to him. 'I think you should have this back. It's a family heirloom and I'm not family.' Or ever will be.

His eyes hardened to ice, his jaw set in stone. 'Keep it. I don't want it.'

Layla curled her fingers around the ring and slipped it into her pocket and silently left the room.

His words could just as easily be referring to her love for him.

Keep it. I don't want it.

Logan forced himself to watch Layla's tail-lights fading into the distance. Forced himself to stand there at the window, watching her leave, instead of racing to his own car and driving after her, begging her to come back. But he was not the sort of man to beg. To plead. To humiliate himself over a relationship that was never going to work. It had all the odds stacked against it from the start and wasn't he the biggest odds of them?

He was the last person to be anyone's godparent. What sort of spiritual guardian would he be? He had messed up big time with his younger brother, keeping the reins too loose, and now he couldn't pull back on them. It was painful to watch his brother self-destruct, knowing he was partly, if not wholly, responsible. He had done an even worse job of taking care of his fiancée. Taking on any more responsibility was asking for another monumental screw-up.

And now he had another one for his personal failure board—his relationship with Layla. It had been doomed from the outset because *he* was the common denominator in all his failed relationships. There was no escaping the uncomfortable truth that he was unable to care for someone without letting them down.

The tail-lights were finally swallowed by the cloaking darkness and he closed the curtains. Hadn't he stood at this very window as a seven-year-old boy, looking for the lights of his mother's car? Every night for a year he had waited, hoping, praying she would return. But, of course, she never had. His mother had told him she loved him every day of his life and yet those words had not brought her back. Her love had not brought her back. It had vanished with her. Or—even more likely—it hadn't been there in the first place.

Layla fancied herself in love with him and he blamed himself for not sticking to his rules. He had blurred the boundaries by taking their relationship from on paper to passion and now he had to pay the price.

But he still had Bellbrae.

Layla had promised not to do anything that would compromise his inheritance and for that he was grateful. To lose Bellbrae would be to lose a big part of himself. He glanced at the Christmas tree that only a short time ago they had decorated together. The porcelain angel on the top of the tree had slipped sideways and looked in danger of falling. He deliberated on whether to climb back up the ladder or leave the angel to its fate. It had been repaired a few times—once Flossie as a puppy had run off with it during the tree-decorating process. Another time Robbie had thrown it in a tantrum not long after their mother had left. It had taken Logan ages to glue it back together before anyone noticed.

Flossie pushed the sitting-room door open with her nose and padded over to him, her tail low, her brown eyes so woebegone it made something in Logan's gut tighten. 'Don't look at me like that,' he said, frowning. 'I didn't ask her to leave.'

But you didn't convince her to stay either.

He pushed aside the intrusive thought and went over to where he had propped the stepladder against the wall. He unfolded the ladder and began climbing but he had only got up three rungs when the angel toppled from the top of the tree and fell to the floor, her porcelain face smashing into pieces no amount of superglue was ever going to fix.

Layla booked herself into a bed and breakfast in Haymarket in the west end of Edinburgh and fell into bed but not into sleep. She lay on her back, eyes streaming with tears, her chest aching with emptiness. What a fool she had been to admit she loved Logan. A gauche fool who should have known better than to think he would ever return her feelings. He had locked away his heart and she had been crazy to think she of all people held the key. She didn't. And never would.

She looked at her bare ring finger and sighed. She'd left his grandmother's engagement ring and her wedding ring on Logan's bedside table. There was no way she could keep his family heirloom. The ring would just have been a painful reminder of how she had failed to win his heart—of how her dreams had been shattered like a robin's egg on concrete.

She picked up her phone and checked if he'd replied to her text informing him she had arrived safely. He had, but in characteristic fashion had kept it brief.

Okay.

No words asking her to reconsider. No words of love. Just 'Okay'.

Layla put the phone back down and flopped back against the pillows with another sigh. More fool her for wanting more than was possible.

But wasn't that the pitiful story of her life?

CHAPTER TWELVE

A WEEK WENT past and Logan swore he could still smell Layla's perfume lingering in the castle. Even when he walked outside to go on one of his long walks over the estate, he thought he could hear the sound of her laugh in the air. And every time the sun peeped out from behind the brooding clouds, he thought of her breath-snatching smile.

Bellbrae was just a deserted old castle without her here. A deserted Highland retreat that was no longer a retreat but more like a prison. He was imprisoned by his thoughts—the thoughts that plagued him day and night, but mostly at night. He would wake from a restless sleep and realised with a jolt that Layla was not sleeping beside him. That her cloud of chestnut hair wasn't splayed out over the pillow, her arms not wrapped around him, her legs not curled close to his.

He'd had to stop using the bedroom he'd shared with her as it contained too many memories. He had even left the engagement and wedding rings on the bedside table where she'd left them. He couldn't bring himself to lock them in the safe because it seemed too…final. Out of sight, out of mind. Except Layla was indeed out of sight but not out of his mind. She was there all the time. He couldn't go through a single minute of the day without thinking of her.

And that's when the pain would start. Pain that spread through his chest like a poison, seeping into his blood and even into his bones. He *ached* with it. He couldn't escape the torment of his body missing hers. But the physical torment he could handle, it was the mental torment he couldn't. The *emotional* torment. Yes, the E word he had scrubbed from his vocabulary a long time ago. Emotions were things he didn't trust, in others but also in himself.

But the emotion he felt now was different. The emptiness he felt was different. The ache inside his chest seemed to be getting worse each day.

Logan had just brought Flossie back in after a comfort walk when he saw his brother's car coming up the driveway. Great. Just what he needed—an uninvited guest at his private pity party.

Robbie parked the car under one of the trees near the old stables. The bare branches waving in the icy wind looked like arthritic fingers.

'God, this place is freezing,' Robbie said, dashing towards Logan with his hand pulling the collar of his coat against his neck.

Logan hadn't noticed the cold. He'd been too preoccupied with missing Layla. 'You didn't tell me you were coming. I would have cranked up the heating.'

Robbie grimaced and followed Logan inside. 'Yeah, sorry about that. But I had my mind on stuff.'

Tell me about it.

Logan led the way to the small sitting room where he had been spending most of his time. Flossie was already in front of the fire with her head on her paws. She wagged her tail across the carpet but didn't go over to greet Robbie.

Robbie pulled one side of his lip into his mouth and shifted his weight from foot to foot. 'Is Layla around? I think it's important she hears what I have to say too, given you guys are married and all. I want to apologise for my behaviour last time. I was unforgivably rude to her.'

Logan walked over to the fireplace and gave the burning coals a poke with the poker. The mention of Layla's name was as painful as if the hot poker had been driven into his chest. 'She's not here.'

'Oh, where is she?'

Logan put the poker back on the fireplace tools rack and faced his brother. 'She left a week ago.'

Robbie frowned. 'Left? Why?'

Logan rubbed a hand down his face and mentally reminded himself to shave sometime. It had been three days at least. 'I suck at relationships, that's why. I hurt people I care about even when I think I'm doing the right thing by them.'

Robbie swallowed a couple of times and sat on the sofa as if his legs were not capable of keeping him upright. He leaned forward and rested his elbows on his thighs and placed his head into his hands.

'Oh, God, this is my fault.' He lifted his head and looked at Logan with a harrowed expression. 'The reason I came here today... I've been to see someone. A psychologist.' He swallowed again and continued, 'I'm not coping with stuff. I haven't been coping for a long time but I've been using other things to take my mind off it. Drinking, the occasional party drug, sex with strangers, so many strangers I've lost count. Gambling.' He groaned and placed his head back in his hands. 'I've lost everything, Logan. Please don't hate me for it. I have nothing left of my trust fund—I've gambled it all away.'

Logan went over to his brother, sat beside him and laid an arm around his quaking shoulders. 'You have me, Robbie. You'll always have me, no matter what.'

Flossie hauled herself up off the carpet in front of the fire and came plodding over to nudge Robbie's thigh, whining as if to say she was there for him too.

Robbie lifted his head out of his hands, his face wet with tears. His hand reached down and scratched behind the dog's ears. 'I want to be a better man. I want to be like you—steady, reliable, responsible. I've been blaming everyone but myself for how I behave, for the stupid choices I've made. But I'm determined to make better choices now. I want to go to rehab. I want to get control of my destructive habits before they hurt the people I love.'

'I'll support you in every way I can,' Logan said.

Robbie leaned back and met Logan's gaze. 'You've always been there for me. I couldn't have asked for a better older brother. You've always had my back and knowing that has kept me from the edge more times than I want to admit. I've let you down so much but I'm determined to change my habits. But what about you and Layla? I can't help thinking I've caused you guys to break up.'

Logan had his own destructive habits to address. The habit of not recognising love, for instance. For not allowing himself to feel it, or receive it. Not trusting love when it was the only thing that kept him going.

Love for his brother, love for Bellbrae and most of all—love for Layla.

Maybe there was hope for him after all. Robbie

had said Logan's love for him had kept him from going over the edge. It gave him hope he might be a better godparent than he'd thought. And who better to be a godparent with than with Layla? The woman he loved with all his heart and soul.

And why stop at godparenting? He started to picture Bellbrae with children sitting around the Christmas tree. The sound of their laughter echoing in the castle and in the gardens and beyond. He and Layla would make an awesome team as parents of their own children. He had loved Layla for so long he had no idea when it had started. It felt like it had always been there inside his heart. Hidden away. Locked away. But he could lock it away no longer.

'No, it wasn't you,' Logan said. 'It was me. I didn't realise how much I loved her until I lost her. I guess it's a bit like you with having to lose everything, having to reach rock bottom before you can resurface, to be reborn.'

Robbie frowned in puzzlement. 'If you love her, then why are you brooding up here all alone?'

Logan sprang from the sofa. 'You're right. I need to go and see her. To tell her I love her exactly the way she wants to be loved. And to bring her back home. Will you be okay looking after Flossie overnight?'

Robbie's face was wreathed in a smile and he turned to look at the dog sitting beside him. 'How about it, Floss? Do you trust me to take care of you while Logan brings back his bride?'

Flossie gave an answering bark and wagged her plumy tail.

Layla was in her office-cum-bedsit in the Old Town of Edinburgh, putting the last touches to the small reception area with a pot plant and new business cards for the counter. Her business name, 'Leave it to Layla and Co', was on a black and gold plaque on the door and another one over the counter. She stepped back to admire her brand-new office space when the door tinkled open behind her.

She turned with a welcoming smile on her face. 'Welcome to...' Her heart jerked sideways in her chest. 'Oh, Logan. Hello...' She licked her lips, a little shocked at his appearance. It looked like he hadn't shaven or slept in days. And his clothes were rumpled as if he'd slept in them—if indeed he had slept. 'Are you okay?'

He closed the door and came over to where she was standing. 'I'm not okay and I'll never be okay without you.' He took her hands in his. 'I love you. I can't tell you when I started loving you. It feels like I've always loved you in one way or another. But it's the way I love you now that's most important.'

Layla's heart began to feel too big for her chest

cavity. It swelled and swelled and she could hardly take a breath or speak. 'You really love me?'

He smiled and hugged her to his chest, resting his chin on top of her head. 'I love you so much I can't find the words to describe it. I would give anything up if it meant I could have you by my side. Even Bellbrae.'

'Oh, Logan,' Layla said, happy tears spilling from her eyes. 'Even Bellbrae?'

He eased back to look down at her with love shining in his gaze. He blotted her tears with the pads of his fingers. 'Even Bellbrae. It's just an isolated and draughty old cold castle without you there. You make it a home. Come back with me and make it a home for both of us. And for any children we might have if we're so lucky.'

'Children?' Layla's eyes widened and her heart just about exploded with joy. 'You want a family?'

'You once pointed out I might need an heir in the future, remember? I can think of no one I'd rather have to be the mother of my children than you. Oh, and by the way, is the invitation to be godfather to little Gabriella still open? I would be honoured to be a godparent with you.'

Layla wound her arms around his neck. 'I can't believe this is happening. I've been so miserable without you. I love you so much.'

He held her close, his arms a strong band around her back. 'When you said I had an emotional limp,

that really resonated with me later. I was too angry
to really understand what you meant at the time.
But it's true. I've been disabled for years by my
fear of failure in a relationship—any relationship. It was as destructive as Robbie's drinking
and gambling. He's getting help, by the way. I'm
so proud of how he's taking that step. He's mind-
ing Flossie while I'm down here sweeping you
off your feet.'

'You are very definitely doing that,' Layla
laughed. 'I don't think my feet will ever touch the
ground again.'

He kissed her long and lovingly, finally raising
his mouth off hers to say, 'Forgive me for hurting
you. For not begging you to stay, and most of all
for not telling you how much I love you.'

Layla stroked his prickly jaw with her hand.
'You've told me now, that's the main thing.'

Logan kissed her hand and then reached into
his coat pocket. 'I was halfway down the driveway at Bellbrae when I realised I'd forgotten to
get your rings. I had to dash back to get them.' He
took out the wedding and engagement rings and
placed them on her left hand. 'There. Back where
they belong.'

Layla's smile threatened to split her face in two.
'I'm so happy I think I'm going to burst. What do
you think of my office? It's a bit on the small side
but it's a start.'

'It looks great. I'm so proud of you, even if I have to confess I'm worried how we're going to juggle our careers. But I'll always support you, no matter what.'

'I've already hired a receptionist to manage the bookings,' Layla said. 'I realise I can't do everything myself. It's not healthy. Besides, I quite like the idea of sleeping in now and again as long as you're there too.'

His eyes glinted and he drew her even closer. 'Come home with me for Christmas?'

Layla lifted her mouth to his. 'Just try and stop me.'

EPILOGUE

Christmas the following year

LOGAN BROUGHT THE tray of mulled wine in for their guests in the sitting room where the Christmas tree was twinkling and the fire roaring in the grate. Rafe and Isla and their adorable twelve-month-old toddler Gabriella were staying for the festive season. Gabby was at the cute cruising around the furniture stage, and every now and again would lose her balance and plonk down on her nappy-clad bottom and smile, showing off her brand new little white teeth.

Aunt Elsie was spending Christmas on a cruise with her pen pal after developing quite a penchant for travelling, but she assured them she would be back when the worst of winter was over.

Robbie was sitting on the opposite sofa with his arm around his new partner Meg, who he'd met in rehab. Logan couldn't believe the difference in his brother. The maturity and acceptance of responsibility had been slow in coming but now it was here, he couldn't have been prouder of the way his brother had addressed his issues.

And then Logan's gaze went to Layla, who was sitting on the third sofa with her feet up on a footstool, cradling their new puppy Rafferty on her lap. Flossie had sadly passed away in her sleep a few months ago and the only way Logan could think to fill the gap the old dog left was to buy Layla a puppy for her birthday. The new angel on the top of the tree already had Raffy's teeth marks on it but thankfully Logan had rescued it in time before more serious damage had been done.

Layla smiled at Logan and his chest filled with warmth. 'Is that the non-alcoholic one?' she asked with a twinkle in her eye that rivalled the Christmas-tree lights.

'I made it specially for you, darling,' Logan said, feeling a rush of love so deep and intense it took his breath away.

'You're not drinking alcohol?' Isla's eyes widened to the size of the baubles on the tree. 'Does this mean…?'

Logan put the drinks tray down and sat beside Layla and placed his arm around her waist. 'Yes, it does. We're expecting a special arrival in June next year.'

'Congratulations!' Rafe and Isla spoke at once and Robbie and Meg soon followed with hugs and kisses.

Even little Gabby wanted to be part of the action and gave them both a sloppy open-mouthed kiss.

'But wait, there's more,' Layla said with a beaming smile that made his heart swell with love. 'We need two sets of godparents. So, will you guys do the honours? Rafe and Isla and Robbie and Meg?'

Robbie's eyebrows shot up. 'You're having twins?'

Logan grinned and hugged Layla close to his side. 'I did say a special arrival, didn't I? Yes, we're having twins.'

* * * * *

Unable to put
Billionaire's Wife on Paper
by Melanie Milburne down?
Find your next page-turner with these other
Conveniently Wed! stories!

Shock Marriage for the Powerful Spaniard
by Cathy Williams
The Innocent's Emergency Wedding
by Natalie Anderson
His Contract Christmas Bride
by Sharon Kendrick
The Greek's Surprise Christmas Bride
by Lynne Graham

Available now!

WE HOPE YOU ENJOYED THIS BOOK!

HARLEQUIN *Presents.*

Get lost in a world of international luxury, where billionaires and royals are sure to satisfy your every fantasy.

Discover eight new books every month, available wherever books are sold!

Harlequin.com

#3789 BOUND BY MY SCANDALOUS PREGNANCY
The Notorious Greek Billionaires
by Maya Blake

Two months ago, I stood outside Neo's office ready to beg forgiveness. Instead, I found myself begging for more, as he set me ablaze with his touch. Now I must tell him I'm pregnant with the child he never expected!

#3790 CROWNED AT THE DESERT KING'S COMMAND
by Jackie Ashenden

The borders of Tariq's kingdom are closed—just like his ironclad heart. After rescuing lost archaeologist Charlotte from the desert, he *can't* let her go. Instead, their mutual desire compels Tariq to crown Charlotte as his queen!

#3791 CRAVING HIS FORBIDDEN INNOCENT
by Louise Fuller

Basa may have almost succumbed to their heated attraction once, but after Mimi's criminal family almost ruined his own, he *won't* be fooled twice. But, thrown together for a society wedding, Basa's fierce control is threatened by her forbidden temptation...

#3792 REDEMPTION OF THE UNTAMED ITALIAN
by Clare Connelly

Cesare is sure one sinful encounter with Jemima will be enough. It's not! Nothing less than claiming her for a red-hot fling will do. But to unravel Jemima's secrets, the Italian must first prove himself worthy of her...

YOU CAN FIND MORE INFORMATION ON UPCOMING HARLEQUIN TITLES, FREE EXCERPTS AND MORE AT HARLEQUIN.COM.

HPCNMRB0120